The

Swere clutching her
he

Sas to come but had no idea
how it.

The continued:

"I think you all know that I have chosen as my new wife the most beautiful woman in England!"

He paused and then continued:

"I therefore ask you to drink a toast to our happiness!"

He raised his glass slowly, obviously delighted with himself for capturing the lovely young Salema.

The others at the table raised their glasses.

The only exceptions were Salema and Charles.

She did not move and neither did he.

Their eyes met across the table and she thought he must see the agony in hers . . .

A Camfield Novel of Love
by Barbara Cartland

Camfield Place,
Hatfield
Hertfordshire,
England

Dearest Reader,

Camfield Novels of Love mark a very exciting era of my books with Jove. They have already published nearly two hundred of my titles since they became my first publisher in America, and now all my original paperback romances in the future will be published exclusively by them.

As you already know, Camfield Place in Hertfordshire is my home, which originally existed in 1275, but was rebuilt in 1867 by the grandfather of Beatrix Potter.

It was here in this lovely house, with the best view in the county, that she wrote *The Tale of Peter Rabbit*. Mr. McGregor's garden is exactly as she described it. The door in the wall that the fat little rabbit could not squeeze underneath and the goldfish pool where the white cat sat twitching its tail are still there.

I had Camfield Place blessed when I came here in 1950 and was so happy with my husband until he died, and now with my children and grandchildren, that I know the atmosphere is filled with love and we have all been very lucky.

It is easy here to write of love and I know you will enjoy the Camfield Novels of Love. Their plots are definitely exciting and the covers very romantic. They come to you, like all my books, with love.

Bless you,

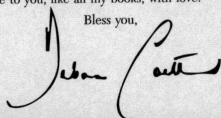

CAMFIELD NOVELS OF LOVE

by Barbara Cartland

A NEW CAMFIELD NOVEL OF LOVE BY

BARBARA CARTLAND

The Cave of Love

J

JOVE BOOKS, NEW YORK

THE CAVE OF LOVE

A Jove Book / published by arrangement with
the author

PRINTING HISTORY
Jove edition / March 1993

ISBN: 0-515-11064-7

Jove Books are published by The Berkley Publishing Group,
200 Madison Avenue, New York, New York 10016.
The name "JOVE" and the "J" logo
are trademarks belonging to Jove Publications, Inc.

PRINTED IN THE UNITED STATES OF AMERICA

10 9 8 7 6 5 4 3 2 1

Author's Note

CAVES have always attracted mankind since the beginning of time.

They were first, of course, used by animals, and the largest cave in England is Giant's Hole, Oxlow, in Derbyshire.

The largest cave in the world is the Mammoth Cave National Park, Kentucky, U.S.A., and was first discovered in 1799.

The caves in Scotland provided hiding-places for the Picts and the Scots when they saw the ships of the Vikings coming across the North Sea to pillage their crops, their animals, and even their women.

Caves hid, romantically, Kings and Pretenders, Pirates and Highwaymen, as well as criminals.

Many a love story has started in a cave and will continue to do so until the world ends.

chapter one

1830

BENDING down and trying vainly to reach her dog, Salema suddenly heard a voice behind her ask:

"What has happened? What are you doing?"

"What do you think I am doing?" she replied crossly. "I am trying to pull my dog out of this terrible hole into which he has fallen!"

The man who had spoken tied the reins of his horse, then, moving beside her, said:

"Let me try."

"Perhaps you will be able to reach him," Salema said. "He is too far down for me, but how could anyone do anything so cruel and so criminal as to dig a hole like this?"

The man who had spoken to her knelt down, then slipped backwards until he was lying on the ground.

Only then could he just reach the neck of the small spaniel who had fallen into the deep, water-logged hole.

1

Slowly he pulled the frightened dog up, needing all his strength to do so until he dragged him out onto the ground.

The girl gave a cry of delight.

"You have done it! You have done it!" she exclaimed. "Oh, thank you, thank you!"

Before she could say any more, the spaniel shook himself violently.

The mud and dirt with which he was covered flew into his mistress's face and bespattered the smart, skilfully tied cravat of his rescuer.

Salema was blinded by the mud.

The man beside her gave a hastily swallowed exclamation of annoyance.

The spaniel moved away, still shaking himself.

Salema wiped her eyes and saw the mud on the Gentleman's cravat.

"I . . . I am sorry . . ." she started to say, groping for a handkerchief.

She did not find one, and the Gentleman pulled one from his pocket.

It was white and clean, and Salema hesitated before she started to wipe her face with it.

"I am so . . . sorry," she said again, "but it is all the fault of the wicked owner of this Wood."

She dabbed her small nose as she spoke, rather ineffectually, leaving a dirty mark across her cheek.

The Gentleman facing her, who was still sitting on the ground, smiled.

Bending forward, he took the handkerchief from her.

"Let me do that," he said.

Like a child, she shut her eyes and raised her face.

Skilfully he wiped the mud from her eye-lids, her cheek, and her chin.

"That is better!" he exclaimed.

He thought, as he spoke, that she was the prettiest girl he had ever seen.

In fact, she was so lovely sitting opposite him, that he could hardly believe he was not imagining her.

The sunshine percolating through the leaves of the trees turned her hair to gold.

Her eyes, now that they were open, seemed to dominate her face.

Strangely enough, they were not blue as they should have been for a perfect English Beauty, but green, flecked with gold.

"I am afraid I have ruined your handkerchief," Salema said.

"In a good cause!" he replied.

He rose to his feet as he spoke and put out his hand to help her up.

He realised as he did so that her riding-habit was an attractive shade of blue.

The white muslin blouse she wore beneath it was also slightly spattered with mud.

She had no hat, and he felt in consequence that she must live somewhere nearby.

As if Salema had read his thoughts, she said:

"Thank you again for your kindness. I should never have managed to rescue Rufus by myself, and the appalling owner of this Estate shoots stray dogs or else leaves them to die in the traps from which you have just rescued him!"

"Can he really be as bad as that?" the Gentleman asked with a slight twist of his lips.

"He is worse!" Salema answered. "And the sooner we get off his land the better!"

She did not wait for the Gentleman to agree.

She walked a little way ahead, then turned inwards.

As she expected, taking the bridle of his horse, the Stranger followed her.

They stepped through a dilapidated fence into another part of the Wood.

Salema still went ahead and a few minutes later came to a clearing.

Her own horse, a very fine-looking Bay, was cropping the grass.

As soon as Salema had started to move away from the hole, Rufus ran after her.

He was still shaking himself from time to time, as if he was determined to get dry.

Now, as Salema reached her own horse, she patted him, then turned to face the Gentleman behind.

"If you take this path," she said, pointing with her finger, "it will take you back to the village, but do remember another time you must never go in His Grace's Wood unless you wish to get into trouble."

"His Grace?" the Gentleman questioned.

"The Duke of Mountaired," Salema said. "He owns a great many acres round here, all of which are strictly taboo."

"It sounds very frightening," the Gentleman said.

"It is!" Salema answered. "If the game-keepers catch you and accuse you of poaching, His Grace will do everything in his power to have you transported."

She paused before she went on:

"As I have already said, stray dogs are shot on

sight, and Rufus would never have gone over the boundary if it had not been for a very provocative and delectable-looking lady rabbit!"

The Gentleman laughed.

"So Rufus has a roving eye!" he remarked.

"Of course he has!" Salema agreed. "And when I bring him here another time, I shall put him on a lead."

She drew in her breath as if remembering what had happened to him, and said again:

"Thank you, thank you! I do not know what I would have done if you had not appeared like a Genie at exactly the right moment to help me."

"I am glad to have been of service," the Gentleman remarked.

He did not, however, mount his horse.

As Salema looked at him questioningly he added:

"I am, of course, interested and intrigued by what you have been saying. Surely there is somewhere where we can sit down and talk without the ground crumbling under us?"

Salema laughed.

"You are quite safe here," she said. "This is 'No-Man's-Land,' although in fact its name is 'Monk's Wood.' "

"Tell me about it," the Gentleman pleaded.

Salema hesitated.

Then, as if she felt she owed him something for saving Rufus, she said:

"If we walk a little farther we shall not only be safer, but you shall see why from there the Wood got its name."

"I would like that," the Gentleman said.

Salema smiled at him.

Taking her horse *Flash* by the bridle, she led him down a narrow, twisting path.

It was in a different direction from the one she had indicated to the Gentleman.

It took her only a few minutes to reach what remained of the Chapel.

It was here an ancient Monk had built himself a place to live following his retirement from the local Priory.

The latter had long since been demolished.

Surprisingly, the Monk's small Chapel in which he had lived and slept still had two of its walls left and part of the roof.

In front of it was a forest pool and a small amount of grass on which the sapling trees never grew.

It was a very attractive site.

As Salema reached it, she let *Flash* loose while Rufus ran forward to drink from the pool.

"So this is where the Monk hid himself from the world!" the Gentleman said.

As he spoke, he released his own horse which joined *Flash* in cropping the grass.

There was the trunk of a fallen tree beside what was left of the Monk's Chapel.

Salema sat on it, and the Gentleman joined her, saying as he did so:

"Tell me—why do you call this 'No-Man's-Land'?"

Salema smiled.

"About six years ago," she explained, "a terrible row broke out between the Duke, who is the greatest Landowner in the County, and the owner of a quite small Estate which marches with his acres."

She paused before she continued:

"They both claimed Monk's Wood, the Duke because he said it rounded off that particular part of his Estate, while the Earl who owned the smaller acreage proclaimed that the Priory from which the Monk came was on his land."

"So what happened?" the Gentleman enquired.

"They raged at each other until finally, rather than have a scandal in the Courts, it was agreed by their Solicitors that the land should belong to neither. In consequence, it is a sanctuary for birds and beasts who live here."

As she spoke, she looked up at the trees above them.

The Gentleman heard a flutter of wings, as if those who were listening were agreeing with what she said.

"So that is why you come here!" he said.

"I am perhaps the only person who does," Salema replied, "for the simple reason that the villagers think it is haunted by the Monk, and the game-keepers on either side walk by, grinding their teeth at the magpies."

She stopped for a moment and smiled at him.

"The squirrels, the pheasants, and the ducks who want a quiet place for their drays and nests all come here and remain unmolested."

"What an extraordinary story!" the Gentleman exclaimed. "I quite understand why it attracts you."

He thought as he spoke that she was so lovely that she might be a Nymph from the pool which lay in front of him.

Or perhaps a Spirit from the trees.

"I come here whenever I feel unhappy," Salema

said. "No-one disturbs me because they have no idea where I am."

"I think that is what everybody wants in their life," the Gentleman said. "Somewhere where they can think and get away from the crowd of chattering tongues which seldom say anything worth listening to."

Salema laughed.

"Now you are being cynical," she said, "and there is no reason to be cynical when one can listen to the birds and the bees and hear the squirrels telling one a tale of adventure and excitement while they hide their nuts."

The Gentleman laughed.

"And what do you think about when you are here?"

"I think about all those who are here with me," Salema replied, "then I travel with the birds when they migrate for the Winter and listen to the tales of the ducks when they fly in from the North because it is too cold there."

"I have been travelling through foreign lands," the Stranger said, "but now I am wondering in my search for new places and new people if I have not missed something in England."

"But you have been able to travel," Salema said. "That is what I long to do, but for the moment I can do so only in my mind."

"If you could travel, where would you go?"

"The world is a big place," Salema answered, "and I would like to see all of it, but I would be quite content to visit the Greek islands, then perhaps a desert in North Africa and look in at the Pyramids of Egypt."

The Stranger laughed.

"That will certainly take you some time."

"I read everything I can find about those countries and a dozen more," Salema said, "but unlike you, it has to be part of my dreams, for I cannot do it in reality."

She paused for a moment, then she said:

"Please tell me about the places you have visited, especially those in the East."

The Gentleman started to describe India, where he had spent some time, to her.

She listened, entranced.

"How could you look at the Himalayas and leave them?" she asked. "I want to see them perhaps more than any other mountains."

"I am sure you believe in the gods who do not allow mere men to explore them," the Gentleman said. "In fact, they are very resentful and cruel to those who try."

"I would be content just to look, marvel, and, of course, worship them," Salema said softly.

They went on talking, until suddenly she gave a little cry.

"It is growing late and I must go! My Mother will be wondering what has happened to me."

"You cannot leave just like that," the Gentleman said. "You must tell me when I can meet you again."

"I do not think that is possible," Salema answered.

"Not possible?" he queried, "but—why?"

"Well, for one thing . . . we have . . . not been . . . introduced!"

The Gentleman laughed.

"We were introduced, whether it was formal or

informal, by Rufus! And do not forget—you have not given me back my handkerchief!"

Salema put her hand into her pocket.

She realised now that the handkerchief was there, but very wet and dirty.

"I will have it washed," she promised, "and return it to you to-morrow."

"You will come here? At what time?" the Gentleman enquired.

Salema thought for a moment.

"At eleven o'clock, if I can get away. But now I really must go!"

She rose from the log on which she was sitting and walked towards her horse.

The Gentleman went with her.

When they reached *Flash* Salema realised he was going to lift her into the saddle.

She smiled at him and said:

"Thank you again for everything, including the loan of your handkerchief. Do you think you will be able to find your way without going on the Duke's land?"

"I am sure I can," the Gentleman replied.

Then, as she waited for him to lift her into the saddle, he said:

"I suppose you realise that although we have been formally introduced, I do not know your name."

Salema thought quickly.

Because she had talked somewhat indiscreetly about the Duke and the feud over Monk's Wood, she thought it would be a mistake for the Stranger to know who she was.

She could, in fact, have given quite a variety of names.

She had been christened Lettice Alverline Harriet Muriel after each one of her Godmothers.

Her Mother had wanted her to be called Salema, thinking it a pretty name and knowing it meant "Peace."

Her Father had reacted violently to the idea.

"What sort of name is that?" he asked. "Some Eastern nonsense! I will not have it in *my* Family Tree!"

His daughter had therefore been christened with the names of which he approved.

Nevertheless, her Mother called her Salema, and it was the name which she herself preferred.

It always seemed to her to fit in with Monk's Wood and the joy she found there.

Now she said:

"My name is Salema. What is yours?"

"It is Charles," the Gentleman replied.

"Charles II was always one of my favourite Kings," Salema remarked.

"Because he was a Roué?" the Gentleman asked with a smile.

"No, because he was very intelligent," she replied, "and loved everything that was beautiful. Do not forget that it was he who put the ducks in the lake at St. James's Park."

The Gentleman laughed.

"That I did not know until now, but of course it is delightful to think he added anything so attractive to London besides the beautiful women who filled his Court."

There was a twinkle in his eyes as he looked at Salema.

It made her suddenly feel shy.

"I must go!" she said, quickly turning towards *Flash*.

Charles lifted her into the saddle.

"I will be waiting here for you to-morrow," he said, "and I shall be very disappointed if you do not come. In fact, like the Monk, I shall haunt this place until I find you again."

"I promise I will be here at eleven o'clock, unless something untoward occurs," Salema replied.

She touched *Flash* with her heel as she spoke, and he started forward.

Charles watched her until she was out of sight amongst the trees.

Then with a sigh he undid the knot he had made in his horse's reins and swung himself onto his back.

He rode away down the path that Salema had indicated to him.

He knew that it would bring him to the small village of Little Bemberry.

* * *

As soon as she had passed out of Monk's Wood, Salema started to ride as quickly as she could.

She had not told the Stranger that her father was the Earl of Ledgebourne simply because she felt she had been indiscreet in saying what she had about the Duke of Mountaired.

All her life, it seemed to her, she had been hearing about the autocratic way in which the Duke ran his Estate.

She knew the hole into which Rufus had fallen was only one of a number of traps which the game-keepers had set for poachers.

They had at one time used the man-traps that crushed the intruders' legs, whether man or beast.

But these were so dangerous that, after two village boys were made lame for life, the villagers had sent a deputation to the Duke.

They demanded that such lethal objects should not be used on his Estate.

He had replied that he would do as he liked on his own land.

At the same time, the feeling against his gamekeepers became so intense that he modified his punishment for the poachers.

Instead of man-traps, he dug deep holes which were invisible until somebody fell into them.

They were not imprisoned by the sharp teeth of a man-trap, but by the hole itself.

When it was filled with mud and water it could be a very disagreeable place in which to spend several hours, let alone days and nights.

One boy was caught in this way while trying to capture a rabbit.

He was lost for three days and nights before he was finally found half-dead with cold and hunger.

After that the Duke had few poachers, but was violently hated by his tenants.

Also by most of the County.

Of course socially they kowtowed to him.

He was rich, he was the Lord Lieutenant, and it was in fact impossible for them to avoid him.

Following the trouble over Monk's Wood, Salema's Father refused to speak to the Duke.

He was as vitriolic about him as any of his tenants.

At the same time, Salema was aware that her

Father was jealous of the position the Duke occupied in the County.

He was the Patron, the President, or Chairman of anything that was important to the people of Hertfordshire.

When the two Landowners met, which was inevitable, they each pretended the other man did not exist.

"If you ask me," Salema's Mother said, "I think they are both behaving in a very childish manner. But, as you are well aware, Darling, there is no use talking to your Father. When he gets an idea into his head, nothing will move it."

Salema knew this was true.

She therefore never mentioned the Duke at home and, like her Father, tried to pretend he did not exist.

Now she felt she had been extremely indiscreet about him to a perfect stranger.

She only hoped he would not find out who she was and repeat what she had said.

'To him I am just Salema,' she thought.

To everybody else in the County she was Lady Lettice.

It was the name she disliked the most of all of those with which she had been christened.

"It always makes me think of rabbits!" she complained to her mother. "And who wants to be named after a vegetable?"

"Your Godmother, Lettice, gave you a very pretty necklace, dearest," the Countess answered, "and has promised to give a Ball for you when you make your *début*."

Salema had looked forward to the Ball.

But disaster had struck two days after she

had been presented to the King and Queen at Buckingham Palace.

With a great deal of grumbling because it was so expensive, her Father had taken her to London.

He had opened Ledgebourne House in Berkeley Square.

It had been closed for years.

He planned to give a small Ball there.

Salema had counted on the promise of one of her Godmothers and perhaps a Reception at which her Grandmother would be the hostess.

The very day after she had been an undoubted success at Buckingham Palace, her maternal Grandmother had died.

The Earl, with a sigh of relief, had returned to the country.

Naturally the whole household, together with Salema, went with him.

"It is too disappointing!" Salema's Mother said miserably.

"I know! I know!" the Earl said sharply. "But nothing can be done about it, and I am not spending any more money on black. Apart from the gowns you and Salema will wear at the Funeral, you can wear your other clothes at home, where nobody will see you."

Salema thought that was some consolation.

At the same time, she felt as if having to leave London was like having the Gates of Paradise closed against her.

She lived a very lonely life in Hertfordshire.

They were near enough to London for the young people to go there to enjoy themselves rather than in the country.

The young men certainly gravitated automatically to the amusing Clubs in St. James's Street, besides enjoying the glittering beauty of the dancers at Covent Garden.

With the death of George IV, a new era began when his brother William came to the throne.

The first thing the new Monarch did was to cut down the extravagances which had been condemned by the prudent.

Yet they had certainly been enjoyed by the great majority of the Social *Beau Ton.*

King William and his prudish young wife, Queen Adelaide, dispensed with three of the Royal Yachts, the foreign musicians, and the French Chefs.

They also dispensed with most of the frivolities at Court as quickly as they could.

"You are missing nothing," one of the young women from Hertfordshire who was still enjoying the Season in London told Salema.

At the same time, she felt she would rather have been able to judge for herself.

Now, as she rode home, she thought it strange that a young man so smartly dressed should be riding about the countryside, unless, of course, he was staying with a neighbour.

She wished now that she had asked him exactly who he was, in which case, she would have to tell him her own name—and that might be uncomfortable.

Her Mother had said to her often enough:

"I know, Darling, you disapprove of the way the Duke treats the poachers, and so does your Father. But it would be a great mistake for you to add fuel to a fire which is already blazing."

Salema had agreed.

"I know, Mama, but I went to see little Billy Cottell, and he is still lame after that ghastly man-trap crushed his leg."

The Countess sighed.

"It is wicked for anyone to use such horrible contraptions," she said, "but the Duke is a very important man, and I do not want him to dislike your Father and his family any more than he does already."

Salema had looked at her Mother in surprise.

"Do you think it could hurt Papa?"

"Of course it could—in quite a number of ways," her Mother said. "As it is, your Father does not have the authority he should because the Duke always over-shadows him."

Salema was sensible enough to realise this was true.

Now she thought she had been very stupid in saying what she had to the Stranger.

At the same time, she had been so upset about Rufus.

If the Stranger had not pulled him out of the hole, she would have had to run to the village for help.

Perhaps, in the meantime, the keepers might have come and shot him.

Salema loved Rufus. He was part of her life, just as *Flash* was her closest companion.

She loved him more than she had ever loved any of her friends.

The house in which she lived came in sight.

She thought it looked very attractive, although not nearly so impressive or important-looking as the Duke's Castle.

Her house was large and apt to be very expensive.

She knew her Father was not a rich man and what he had was spent on his race-horses.

It was the Earl's greatest pleasure.

Although he had only a few, they had done remarkably well over the last two seasons.

Even at this moment he was attending Royal Ascot.

Of course neither she nor her Mother could go there this year, as they were in mourning.

"I do hope, Mama, that Papa wins several races!" Salema had said this morning. "Otherwise he will be very cross when he comes home. His best mare, of which he had such high hopes, has not produced a particularly good foal."

"I warned your Father," her mother replied, "that the stallion was not good enough, but of course he would not listen."

Salema's Mother was a very gentle woman.

She had realised soon after she was married that it would be quite useless to oppose her husband in any way.

She had therefore agreed with everything he said, then gone her own way.

She read innumerable books and embroidered the most exquisite cushions for the chairs.

She filled the house with flowers.

She did not listen when her husband complained forcefully and aggressively at every difficulty which occurred day by day.

Salema would understand why she had chosen her own name because it meant "Peace."

It was something she felt her Mother had been seeking all through her married life.

She reached the house and turned towards the stables.

It was a long-drawn-out battle between her and her Father as to whether she should ride alone, or be accompanied by a groom.

Because she usually wanted to go to Monk's Wood, she insisted on being alone.

It was easier when her Father was away.

There were no reproaches or the inevitable argument that "a young lady should be accompanied by a groom!"

'If I am to meet Charles to-morrow,' she thought, 'I certainly do not want anybody with me.'

She gave *Flash* over to a groom and hurried into the house.

Finding her lady's-maid there, she asked her to wash the Gentleman's handkerchief.

"However did you get this in such a mess, M'Lady?" the maid asked.

"It was Rufus's fault. He fell into a dirty pool, then shook himself all over me!" Salema replied.

"It's gone all over Your Ladyship's white blouse!" the maid said. "And a nice job I'll have trying to get that clean!"

"I am sorry," Salema replied, "but it could not be helped."

She changed her clothing.

Then she ran down the stairs to the Drawing-Room, where she knew her Mother would be having tea.

"I am sorry to be late, Mama," she said, "but it was such a lovely day that I forgot the time."

"I thought that was why you had not returned," the Countess said. "I can see the ride has done you good. There is colour in your cheeks and your eyes are shining."

It occurred to Salema that this might be because she had experienced an adventure.

Of course it had been an adventure to meet the Gentleman who had rescued Rufus.

He had talked to her of India, of the Himalayas and the Ganges, all of which she so longed to visit.

He had also been to Greece.

She thought she must get him to tell her more about the "Shining Cliffs" of Delphi and the ruined Temples which were only now being discovered by the Archaeologists.

'It is tiresome being a woman!' she thought to herself as she sat down at the tea-table. 'If I were a man I could go round the world and no-one would think it at all extraordinary. If I want to go as far as St. Albans to buy some ribbon, there is a commotion about it!'

"I have a new book from London," her Mother was saying, "and I know you will find it interesting."

"What is it about, Mama?"

"It was written by a man who has recently travelled across the Sahara Desert."

Salema gave a little cry of delight.

"Oh, Mama, that will really be exciting! Please, read quickly so that I can read it after you."

Her Mother smiled.

"If you like, I will be unselfish and let you have it first. I have not yet finished the book I was reading about Japan."

"Do you ever wish that you were rich, Mama, so that you could go to these places yourself," Salema asked, "instead of just sitting here among the cabbages?"

Her Mother laughed.

"It is not as bad as that, but I know what you mean. The answer is, of course I would like to see these wonderful places for myself, especially the Palaces."

She paused and then continued:

"But being discontented gets us nowhere, and anyway, I am now too old and too weak to travel any farther than London."

Salema did not protest.

She knew that her Mother was very fragile.

It was one of the great sorrows of her Father's life and why he was often disagreeable that he had no son.

He had been delighted when she had been born, but would have preferred her to have been a boy.

After Salema his wife had two children in quick succession, but both were stillborn.

It was then the doctors said there could be no more.

There was nothing the Earl of Ledgebourne could do about it.

Of course he was desperately disappointed.

His wife did everything she could to try and make up to him for it.

Yet she knew it was a bitter blow.

"You must try not to upset Papa," she had said to Salema when she was very young, "and if he is cross with you, it is because you were not the boy he so much wanted."

"Why should he want me to be a boy, Mama?" Salema asked.

"Every man wants a son to follow in his footsteps," her Mother answered, "and of course your Father has a title—a very old one. Because he has no son, it will go to a Cousin he has never liked."

Salema had been quite young when she understood how much this mattered.

She had tried in her own way to make up for the brother she did not have.

She rode with her Father until the grooms said she was as good as any boy in taking the highest fences.

She learnt to shoot not only with a bow and arrow but with a duelling pistol.

Now she could hit the bull's-eye of the target every time.

But she knew that whenever her Father looked at the Family Tree which hung framed on the wall in his Study, he winced.

Beneath his name was only hers and not that of a son.

"I do hope Papa has won at Ascot!" she said aloud.

"I have been praying that he will," he mother replied. "I am sure *Shining Star* has a chance of winning the Gold Cup."

"All the best horses will be competing against him," Salema said, "including the Duke's."

"If the Duke's horse beats Papa's, he will mind more than if it is anyone else's. Oh, Salema, do you really think he has a chance?"

"They were saying in the stables that the Duke is confident he is going to win with *Victorious*. He is a very fine stallion with Arab blood in him."

The Countess looked unhappy.

Salema, rising from the table, went and knelt beside her Mother.

"Do not worry, Mama," she said. "There is nothing we can do about it, but I only wish we had some good news to tell Papa when he comes home to-morrow."

"You are quite sure that the foal born this morning is no good?" her Mother asked.

Salema shook her head.

"I am afraid not. What Papa really wants is a stallion like *Shining Star*."

The Countess gave a little cry.

"That would be terribly expensive! Oh, Darling, do not suggest it—not at the moment, when Papa has had the extra expense of going to London, and all to no avail."

"Of course I will say nothing," Salema agreed.

"I know it is disappointing for you," her Mother said. "We might have been at Royal Ascot instead of sitting here with nothing to do."

"Well, at least Papa could go," Salema said. "It does not seem fair, does it, that he does not have to be in mourning while we do!"

The Countess smiled.

"Men always have the best of everything! Surely, Darling, you realise that by this time?"

"I suppose so," Salema said, "but it is not fair. I was thinking, riding home just now, that I would like to be a boy and climb the Himalayas."

There was a little silence.

Then the Countess said:

"I think we all have 'Himalayas' in our lives, and if we are brave and determined, we manage to climb them, some way or another."

chapter two

SALEMA awoke with a feeling of excitement.

She knew this morning she would see Charles again.

It was a change from the monotony of riding alone or with her Father.

She was aware that her Mother would consider it very reprehensible for her to be meeting a stranger.

But, she told herself, if it had not been for him, she would have been in tears because of Rufus.

'He is kind and he is very strong,' she thought.

Her Mother always had breakfast in bed, and Salema breakfasted alone.

There were various things she always did in the morning.

She arranged the flowers and made sure those she had put in vases yesterday had plenty of water.

Then at last she could run upstairs and put on her riding-habit.

On her dressing-table, just as she expected, was the handkerchief belonging to Charles.

Her maid had washed and ironed it.

It was clean, white, and, she realised, made of fine, expensive linen.

She wondered again who he could be and what he was doing in Little Bemberry?

Strangers were few and far between unless they were calling to see her Father or the Duke.

Then they were usually elderly men.

Where the Duke was concerned, his visitors were Statesmen, Politicians, or Noblemen, and were recognised by the villagers.

This was always an excitement, and gave them something to talk about.

It was half-past-ten when she mounted *Flash*.

She set off across the fields, thinking perhaps she would be early.

At the same time, she was aware that she was excited and eager to see Charles again.

He was so interesting about his travels, she thought.

She wished she could tell her Mother the things he had told her.

She reached Monk's Wood and, as usual, there seemed to be more birds and rabbits there than anywhere else.

She rode through the dilapidated hedge which no-one had bothered to repair.

A mossy patch curved and twisted amongst the fir-trees.

Turning towards the ruined Chapel, she saw Charles's horse and felt her heart turn a somersault.

He was there!

He was waiting for her and she had been half-afraid that he would have forgotten.

He might have had to leave wherever he was staying and return to London.

But he was there!

She rode into the clearing and saw him sitting on the fallen tree-trunk, waiting for her.

She slid down from the saddle before he could reach her.

"You have come!" he exclaimed. "I was beginning to think I had imagined you, or that you had slipped away into the pool and all I would see would be your reflection in the water!"

Salema laughed.

"I am here," she said, "and I have brought you your handkerchief, white and clean as it was before you used it to wipe the mud from my face."

She took the handkerchief from her pocket and handed it to him.

"Thank you," he said, "and may I say how lovely you look this morning without that mud on your cheek."

Because he spoke in a deep voice and not jokingly, Salema felt herself blush.

They walked slowly towards the tree-trunk, leaving the horses to crop the grass beside the pool.

Because she had ridden so fast in her eagerness to get to Monk's Wood, Salema felt hot.

She took off her jacket and laid it beside her on the trunk.

She saw that Charles was looking at her white blouse with its insets of lace and hoped he admired her.

She had taken extra pains at arranging her hair this morning.

The blouse she was wearing was her best and

had been purchased in Bond Street.

Then, as she glanced at Charles, she realised that he was looking at her in a manner which was somehow different from the way he had done so yesterday.

"What is it?" she asked. "What is . . . wrong?"

"Nothing is wrong," he replied, "except that I have been awake most of the night thinking about you and wondering if it was possible that you could be as beautiful as I remembered."

Salema blushed again.

Looking away from him, she said in a shy little voice:

"I . . . I do not think you . . . should talk to me . . . like that!"

"Why not?" Charles enquired.

"Because you are a . . . stranger and I know . . . nothing about you."

He smiled.

"Surely that is what makes it so interesting. We know a great deal about each other, but not the dull, banal things which we would know if we had met in somebody's Drawing-Room, or perhaps at a Ball where the chaperons were sitting on the dais, looking disapprovingly at everything we did."

Salema thought that he was quite right.

Of course it was more exciting that they had met when he had saved Rufus.

They had talked by the magic pool in Monk's Wood with no-one to disapprove of them except the birds.

Charles read her thoughts.

"We think the same things," he said, "and we

understand each other, so whatever happens we must not spoil that."

"No . . . of course . . . not," Salema agreed.

"I wanted to come here this morning," Charles said, "because you are different and because the most exciting thing that has happened to me for a long time was meeting you."

Salema knew that she felt the same.

She felt a little quiver go through her body because of the way he was speaking.

"You are right," he said, "this is like a Fairy Story and we must not spoil it. That is why I wanted you to meet me here alone and talk to you about the things that matter to both of us that have nothing to do with the troubles and difficulties of the world outside."

"I am glad you think it is a very special place," Salema said.

"And you are a very special person," Charles said, "and because this is where you belong, you must not let anyone spoil Monk's Wood—or you!"

Because he was speaking in such a serious voice, Salema turned to look at him.

Then, as their eyes met, it was impossible for either of them to look away.

For a moment, or it might have been a century, they just looked into each other's eyes.

The rest of the world had vanished.

Then Charles said in a very strange voice:

"Oh, my dear, I am afraid of my own feelings, and it is impossible to put them into words."

Because he spoke, it broke the spell and Salema was able to look away from him.

Staring at the horses, although she did not really

see them, she said after a moment:

"I . . . I cannot stay for long. My Father is coming home this morning and . . . he will be angry if I am not there to greet him when he arrives."

"I have to see you again," Charles said. "What are you doing this afternoon?"

"I expect I shall be with Papa. He may have some important things to do . . . or people to see."

"Then I shall wait here," Charles said.

"It might be . . . impossible for me to . . . get away."

"Then what about to-morrow morning?"

"I always ride with Papa in the mornings."

Unexpectedly, Charles reached out and took her hand.

"Listen," he said, "I know there are a thousand reasons why you cannot do something, but there is one reason that is more important than all the rest, and it is that we have to see each other."

As he touched her, Salema felt again that strange little quiver.

He looked down at her hand, then very gently took it in both of his and turned it over.

He looked at the lines on the softness of her palm and asked:

"Shall I tell you your future?"

"Can you do that? I thought you were a Genie, not a Magician."

"I think your future is very easy to read," Charles said. "You will have to make a choice between the conventional and the unconventional, and it is hard to predict which you will choose."

It was difficult for Salema to understand what

he was saying simply because both his hands were touching hers.

"You are so beautiful," he said, "that you may be offered a throne or it may be something very simple like a cave in the mountains."

He traced the lines on her hand with his fingers, and Salema felt as if he mesmerised her.

In a very small voice that seemed to come from a long way away she said:

"I think the . . . choice will rest on . . . who sits on the throne beside me . . . and who is . . . in the . . . cave."

"That is just the answer you ought to make," Charles said. "But what is important is, whichever you choose, it should bring you happiness and of course—love."

As he spoke the last word he raised her hand in both of his and kissed the palm very gently.

It was something that had never happened to Salema before.

As his lips touched her skin she felt as if the sunshine streaked through her body.

It gave her an ecstasy she had never known.

Then, because she was shy, she took away her hand and rose to her feet.

"I must go . . . I really . . . must go," she said.

For a moment Charles did not rise, but just sat looking at her.

The sunshine was turning her hair to gold.

Because he had aroused strange emotions within her, her lips trembled a little and there was a flush of colour on both her cheeks.

"Must you leave me?" he asked.

"I . . . I have . . . to."

"But you would like to stay? Tell me you would like to stay."

"I would like to talk to you," she said. "I was thinking last night of all the exciting things you told me which were different from anything I have ever heard before."

"Then somehow we must meet," Charles said.

"I will try . . . I really will try . . . but I do not want . . . you to wait in case I . . . cannot come . . . to you."

"I will wait!" he said.

He rose to his feet.

He seemed very tall and overwhelming silhouetted around the trees.

She looked up at him.

Very slowly, as if he savoured the moment, he put his arms around her.

It was not what she had expected him to do.

Yet, as he drew her close, it seemed inevitable and something which had been planned since the beginning of time.

He drew her closer still, then his lips were on hers.

He kissed her gently, as if she were something very precious and hardly human and he was half-afraid that, like "Fairy Gold," she would vanish at the touch of his hands.

Then, as he felt the softness and innocence of her lips, his kiss became more possessive.

To Salema it was as if the sunshine were rising through her body.

It turned the whole world into something so incredibly beautiful and wonderful that it could not be real.

She had always thought that being kissed would be marvellous if it was with somebody one loved.

And yet the kiss that Charles was giving her was even more wonderful and more rapturous than she had ever imagined.

Only when he released her did she say a little incoherently:

"Y-you should not have . . . done that! I am . . . sure you should . . . not have . . . kissed me!"

"How could I help it?" Charles asked.

He would have pulled her to him again, but, because she wanted him to, she ran away to find *Flash*.

She was standing with her hand on the bridle with her back to Charles.

He walked towards her very slowly.

When she became aware of him standing behind her, she said in a very small voice:

"Please . . . Charles . . . I must . . . go!"

"I know that," he said, "but promise you will come back here either this afternoon or to-morrow morning?"

"I . . . I will try . . . I really will . . . try."

She did not turn round as she spoke.

Resolutely, as if he forced himself to do so, he picked her up and lifted her into the saddle.

She picked up the reins and looked down at him.

"Remember," he said, "I shall be waiting, and thinking of you every second until I see you again."

Salema knew she would be doing the same.

But it was something she could not say.

Instead, she only looked into his eyes.

Then, although it was an agony to leave him, she urged *Flash* forward.

He carried her on the path down which they had come.

Charles stood still and watched her go.

Salema wanted to look at him, but she was afraid to do so in case he was no longer looking at her.

She reached the end of the Wood, where it opened out onto a field.

Then she felt as if she were leaving something very, very precious behind her.

Perhaps she would never find it again.

"I will be able to see him again this afternoon," she told herself reassuringly, "even if it is only for a few minutes."

Then, because she was frightened of her own thoughts, she pushed *Flash* into a gallop.

Yet she felt that her heart had been left behind in the Wood.

"I *must* see him . . . I *must!*" she told herself.

She could still feel his lips holding hers captive.

* * *

The Jockey Club box was full.

There was that strange quiet as the crowd watched the horses coming down the straight towards the winning-post.

There were two favourites and the Bookies had made short odds on both of them.

Victorious, which belonged to the Duke of Mountaired was 3–1 on.

Shining Star, whose owner was the Earl of Ledgebourne, was 2–1 on.

Both owners had pushed their way to the front of the stand and had binoculars up to their eyes.

The favourites were neck and neck as they came round the bend and accelerated their pace.

It was easy to decipher the yellow cross lines over the green blouse, which were the Duke's colours.

Blue and claret were the Earl's.

The two horses, having pulled out from the pack behind them, were tearing down the turf.

Both owners found it difficult to see if there was so much as an inch between them.

"Come on! Come on, damn you!" the Duke murmured under his breath.

The Earl was finding it hard to breathe.

Then, when they were only a short distance from the winning-post, the unexpected happened.

An outsider came swinging out from the rails.

Riding between the two leading horses, he appeared to separate them as if by magic.

Forcing his way forward, the jockey took his horse past the winning-post half a length ahead of them.

It all happened so quickly and unexpectedly.

The on-lookers hardly had time to gasp before it was realised that the two favourites had been beaten.

A complete outsider which, for the moment no one even recognised, had won.

It was the Duke who exclaimed furiously:

"Swinton, by God! He should be disqualified!"

"I agree with you," the Earl said without thinking to whom he was speaking. "The man was clearly bumping and boring, and we should object!"

"It is something I intend to do!" the Duke said angrily.

He then realised that quite a number of the members of the Jockey Club were clapping their hands and cheering.

Now Lord Swinton's horse was coming back towards the enclosure.

"Well done!" "Well ridden!" "A damned good race!" they were shouting.

The Earl remembered that Lord Swinton was a very popular personality who had distinguished himself in various different ways.

He had then taken up horse-racing late in life.

He had many friends, not only at Court, but also in the Clubs of St. James's.

He was chairman of several Charities on which he spent so much of his time and money.

The Earl knew that to attack Lord Swinton would undoubtedly be a very unpopular move.

If the Judges had decided he had won the race, there was nothing either he or the Duke could do about it.

Even as he thought this, the number of Swinton's horse went up on the board.

There was no doubt that Number Nine was the winner.

"Disgraceful! Utterly disgraceful!" the Duke was grumbling. "Anyone but a blind man would have seen that the way the jockey separated our horses was a definite infringement of the rules!"

"That is true," the Earl agreed, "but, I think, Your Grace, it would be a mistake for us to say so."

He had to speak rather loudly because the cheers of the crowd surging round the winning horse were almost deafening.

As the betting had been 16–1, it was obvious that the Bookies had made a killing.

Those who had been fortunate enough to back the horse because they liked its owner were delighted.

Other numbers were going up on the board—six and four, those of the Duke and the Earl's horses.

They had obviously jointly achieved second place.

The Duke looked at the figures with a jaundiced eye.

"A dead heat!" he exclaimed. "And we would have had the pleasure of winning the Gold Cup if Swinton had not snatched it from our grasp in that outrageous fashion!"

"I agree! I agree!" the Earl replied. "I had no idea that he had a horse that could beat *Shining Star!*"

"Or *Victorious!*" the Duke added.

Most of the members of the Jockey Club had hurried from the box to congratulate Lord Swinton.

The Duke and the Earl were left almost alone.

"I suppose we shall have to make the best of it," the Duke said finally, "and I for one could damned well do with a drink!"

"So could I," the Earl agreed as if it had suddenly occurred to him.

The two disgruntled owners walked side by side to the Bar at the back of the box.

"I had imagined that when I came here next I would be celebrating the fact that, after fifteen years, I had at last obtained the Gold Cup."

"I thought the same," the Earl replied, "and I still cannot believe that it has been snatched away in that outrageous manner at the very last minute!"

"I cannot think where Swinton got his Jockey, let alone his horse!" the Duke remarked.

Because he was so upset, he ordered a bottle of champagne and offered a glass to the Earl.

It was only when they were sitting down and the waiter was filling their glasses for the second time that it occurred to the Earl that it was somewhat strange.

After six years of silence he was suddenly speaking to his neighbour.

Aloud he said:

"I suppose really we should go and watch the weighing-in, but I would find it difficult to be polite to Swinton at this moment."

"And I would certainly tell him what I thought of his Jockey's behaviour and the crooked—and I mean crooked—way in which he snatched victory from our hands!" the Duke said furiously.

Now they were the only occupants of the box except for the waiters.

They could still hear the noise, the excitement, and the cheers in the distance.

It meant that Lord Swinton's horse had been weighed in.

"I must, of course," the Earl said, accepting another glass of champagne, "congratulate you on *Victorious*, the most magnificent stallion I have ever seen!"

"That is what I thought myself," the Duke replied, "but I hear you have some very fine mares."

The Earl looked surprised.

"Who told you that?"

The Duke managed a faint smile at the corner of his lips.

"I cannot believe, Ledgebourne," he said, "that anything goes on in my stable that you do not know about, just as I am always told of what is happening in yours!"

The Earl laughed.

"That is true, and as Your Grace is well aware, there is not much else to talk about in Little Bemberry."

There was a pause.

Then, as he permitted his glass to be filled yet again, the Duke said:

"I have had a lot of disappointment with my mares. I would like to have a look at yours."

The Earl could hardly believe what he was hearing.

Then, despite himself, he said:

"I suppose we might produce a horse which would be unbeatable, even by Swinton!"

"That is just what I was thinking," the Duke remarked. "Dammit all! We have to do something in our own defence!"

"I agree with you," the Earl said. "Two of my mares are definitely exceptional, but unfortunately I have not been able to afford to buy a stallion like *Victorious* to serve them."

The Duke made a strange sound which was meant to be a laugh.

"The answer to that is obvious," he said. "If we put *Victorious* together with your mares, we ought, in a few years' time, make Swinton look foolish!"

"That is a certainty," the Earl said as he laughed.

The Duke drank some more champagne before he said:

"I am thinking it would be a mistake for us not to collaborate. After all, we live side by side, so there should be no difficulty about it."

"None!" the Earl agreed.

"I have taken a great deal of trouble over my

horses," the Duke said, "but I have no family who are interested in them, and I have been wondering what will happen to them when I am no longer there."

The Earl looked at the Duke in surprise.

"You have a son," he said.

There was a note in his voice that anyone listening would have known was a bitter one.

"A son!" the Duke snorted. "I have not seen the young scallywag for years! He walked out when I wanted him to go into the family Regiment and God knows what has happened to him now!"

The Earl had heard this discussed many times, and he merely replied:

"But at least you have somebody to take your Estate and title when you die. I have only a daughter."

"I am sorry about that," the Duke said.

This was something he had heard discussed a thousand times over the years.

"She is very beautiful," the Earl said reminiscently, "and was a sensation when she was presented at the first Drawing-Room in April."

"So I heard," the Duke replied.

"But daughters are not the same as sons!" the Earl said sadly.

A waiter brought another bottle of champagne, and the two noblemen went on drinking.

"I suppose," the Earl said in a rather thick voice, "I shall have to be content with having grandsons while my title goes to a Cousin who has never married and whose only interest is in collecting shells!"

"Oh, Gad, what a waste!" the Duke exclaimed.

"My wife could have no more children," the Earl said heavily, determined to make it clear there was nothing he could do.

The Duke was silent.

It was then the Earl remembered that the Duchess had died three years ago.

He wondered if in consequence His Grace was lonely and that was why, for the moment at any rate, they were talking intimately of family matters.

"I have just been thinking," the Duke said slowly, "that if you are waiting for the grandsons you do not yet possess to admire and enjoy your horses, you will have a very long wait!"

The Earl sighed.

"What else can I do?" he asked.

"It suddenly occurred to me," the Duke went on, "and I cannot think why I have not thought of it before, that as things are at the moment I might have another son, perhaps several!"

The Earl turned to stare at him.

"Do you mean you might marry again, Your Grace?"

"Why not?" the Duke answered. "I am not too old, if it comes to that, and it occurred to me that if we are to collaborate over the horses, we might collaborate in another way."

The Earl did not understand, and the Duke explained:

"I am suggesting, Ledgebourne, that I might marry your daughter. From all I have heard, she would certainly grace the Mountaired diamonds, and if *Victorious* and your mares can produce a decent race-horse, I should be able to produce some sons to ride them!"

The Earl gasped.

Then it flashed through his mind that nothing could be more advantageous.

If his daughter were the Duchess of Mountaired, she would be the most important woman in the County.

All the difficulties and disagreeableness between the two Estates would be swept away.

He had hated the Duke while the controversy over Monk's Wood was raging.

Now, however, he was thinking that he was an extremely impressive man.

The Duke had been extraordinarily handsome in his youth.

Now, at fifty-seven, he was still good-looking as well as distinguished.

It took him a moment to find his voice, and when he did he said:

"It is certainly an idea, Your Grace, and I cannot believe that any son of yours would not be as fine as *Victorious.*"

"I should damned-well hope so!" the Duke exclaimed.

They had another glass of champagne before he went on:

"That is settled then. Bring your daughter to dinner to-morrow night and, of course, your wife, if she is well enough, and we will plan everything."

"Yes, of course, Your Grace," the Earl agreed.

"I am leaving now," the Duke said, "I have had enough of this race-meeting with Swinton behaving in that barbarous manner! We shall meet at Windsor Castle at dinner."

"Yes, I suppose so," the Earl said somewhat grimly, "and Swinton will undoubtedly be there."

"Damned if I congratulate him!" the Duke remarked as he walked away.

The Earl, who had risen to his feet, sat down again.

He felt he must be dreaming—or perhaps it was the effect of the champagne.

He could hardly believe that, in the short time after the race was won, he would be talking to the man he had thought of as his worst enemy, the man who now suggested he should marry his daughter and make her a Duchess.

The waiter filled his glass and went away again.

Then, without really thinking what he was doing, the Earl paid for both bottles of champagne.

Finally, thinking that his life had turned upside-down, he walked slowly down to the paddock.

"It cannot be true!" he said as he stumbled through the crowd.

Then, as he reached the paddock, he saw his horse which was entered for the next race being paraded slowly round the enclosure—and knew by the expression on the face of his Manager, who was leading him, how disappointed he was.

Quite suddenly it occurred to him that it did not matter in the slightest that he had not won the Gold Cup.

He had won the Duke as a son-in-law.

It meant the end of a bitter confrontation which had hurt him far more than it had hurt the Duke.

"I am the luckiest man alive!" the Earl of Ledgebourne told himself.

chapter three

As Salema came in sight of the house, she realised that her Father's carriage was standing at the bottom of the steps.

'I am late,' she thought.

She hoped he would not ask too many questions as to where she had been.

She rode as quickly as she could into the stables and left *Flash* with the grooms.

Then she ran into the house.

She hurried through the passages which led to the hall.

As she reached the hall she realised that her Mother was not yet downstairs.

Her Father was talking to the Butler.

She ran forward to greet him, holding out her arms.

"You are back, Papa! How lovely! What happened?"

She asked the question a little nervously.

At the same time, she was aware that her Father

was smiling and talking in a good-humoured voice.

She felt he must have won.

Her Father put his arms around her.

"I am delighted to see you, my dearest," he said. "I have a lot to tell you. Where is your Mother?"

"I am here," the Countess said from the top of the stairs.

She came down slowly.

Her husband waited until she reached the last step, then he kissed her.

"You have taken care of yourself?" he asked.

"I am quite all right," she replied, "but of course Salema and I have been worrying about you."

"Come into the Study," the Earl ordered. "I have a lot to tell you."

He started to leave the hall.

Then, to Salema's surprise, as he passed the Butler he said:

"Bring a bottle of champagne and three glasses."

"Very good, M'Lord."

Salema glanced at her Mother.

They both knew that, if her Father had something to celebrate, it meant that *Shining Star* had won the Gold Cup.

The Earl walked into his special sanctum, where Salema had arranged several vases of flowers.

The sunshine was coming through the windows.

She thought, with relief, that *Shining Star* had won and he would therefore not be thinking about what she had been doing.

The Countess sank down in a comfortable arm-chair.

The Earl stood in front of the fireplace which, as it was summer, was filled with plants.

He was looking at Salema as she walked towards him.

There was an expression in his eyes she did not understand.

"Tell us everything, Papa," she begged. "I feel you have come back with some very good news."

"Very good news indeed," the Earl said. "*Shining Star* came second to tie with *Victorious*."

Salema stared at him.

She knew that *Victorious* was the Duke's horse.

She could not understand why her Father seemed so pleased.

"But who . . . won?" she asked nervously.

"Swinton. I am sorry to say," the Earl replied, "and a more disgraceful and irregular piece of riding I have never seen! Both the Duke and I wished to protest against the result, but it was not possible."

"The Duke?" the Countess questioned. "Do you mean you were speaking to him?"

"We were talking and we both agreed it was the most outrageous and abominable piece of bumping and boring," the Earl replied. "It would have meant disqualification if the Judges were doing their job properly."

Salema was bewildered.

She could not understand why, if this had happened, he was in such a good mood.

She was just about to ask him some questions, when the door opened.

The Butler came in, accompanied by a footman who was carrying a silver tray.

On it there was an ice-bucket containing a bottle of champagne.

He set it down on a table just inside the door.

The Butler filled three glasses which he carried on a salver first to the Countess.

Then he offered a glass to Salema and finally to the Earl.

As they took them, Salema looked at her Mother questioningly.

She realised the Countess was as bewildered as she herself was.

The Earl waited until the servants had left the room.

Then as the door closed behind them he raised his glass.

"To a very successful day at Ascot," he said, "and to my very beautiful daughter!"

Salema's eyes widened.

"Thank you, Papa," she said, "but I am sorry that *Shining Star* did not win the Gold Cup."

"That is immaterial because of what occurred after the race was over."

"What was that?" the Countess asked.

There was silence.

Then it seemed as if the Earl was deliberately thinking of what he could say to make it sound more melodramatic.

After a few minutes, slowly and with his eyes on Salema, he said:

"Our neighbour, the Duke of Mountaired, has asked for my daughter's hand in marriage!"

There was silence.

Both the Countess and Salema seemed as if they had been turned to stone, until, as the Earl drank his champagne, Salema asked:

"Is . . . this a . . . joke, Papa?"

"No, it is a solid fact," the Earl said. "When the Duke and I realised we had been defrauded by Swinton's horse, and when I congratulated him on what a fine stallion *Victorious* was, he told me he had heard I had some outstanding mares."

He paused to drink some more champagne before he continued:

"That was when we decided to collaborate in breeding an exceptionally fine animal which will undoubtedly win the Gold Cup in the future. Swinton or no Swinton."

"Does this mean," the Countess said, trying to clear her mind, "that your ridiculous feud is now over?"

"It is at an end," the Earl replied, "because we not only intend to collaborate with our stables, but in a much closer relationship."

"I . . . I do not . . . understand." Salema said, and her voice trembled.

"The Duke and I were speaking," the Earl said, "of how disappointing it was that I had no son to carry on my title and, of course, to take an interest in my horses—while he has a son who has been a bitter disappointment to him. It appears it suddenly struck him that he was now a widower."

"But of course he is a widower," the Countess remarked as if she were finding it hard to follow what her husband was saying. "The Duchess died three years ago."

"It had not occurred to Mountaired before," the Earl went on, "that he was free to marry again and have other sons as well as the Marquis."

It was then that Salema realised what was coming.

She gripped her fingers together to prevent herself from screaming.

"Mountaired," the Earl said very slowly, "having heard of Salema's success at Buckingham Palace, realises that she would make him a very beautiful Duchess."

"Are you saying that he wants to marry Salema?" the Countess asked. "But he has never seen her!"

"He has heard about her, and there is no doubt that all London has been talking since she was presented."

"But, Papa . . . you cannot be . . . serious?" Salema expostulated. "How can I possibly marry the Duke? I . . . hate everything he . . . stands for . . . his cruelty to . . . the poachers and those terrible man-traps in the woods."

She was thinking if it had not been for Charles, she might never have been able to save Rufus.

"I expect the stories of his behaviour have been exaggerated by the villagers," the Earl said in a lofty way, "and doubtless, when you are married to him you will be able to encourage him to be a little kinder to the poachers, who should not be on his land anyway!"

"But Papa, you yourself have said how badly he has behaved over Monk's Wood! And you know that several small boys have been crippled because of the man-traps he has had set on his Estate."

Salema rose from the chair.

"Am I to understand, Papa, that you have definitely accepted the Duke's suggestion and given your approval to my becoming his wife?"

"Of course! Of course I have!" the Earl said. "As I have already said, you are not likely to get a better offer, and I shall be delighted—yes, delighted, to have Mountaired as my son-in-law. It will make things very different for me in the future from what they have been up to now."

"But . . . I cannot marry . . . him!" Salema cried.

"Do not be so ridiculous!" the Earl argued. "You have not met the man, and when you do you will find him extremely pleasant. He will, I am sure, make you a very devoted husband."

Salema did not speak, and the Earl went on:

"After all, the man is a Gentleman, and whatever tales there are about him, they are just the gossip of villagers who have nothing else to talk about."

He paused for a moment and then said:

"Man-traps, poachers, and village boys! Can you think of nothing else?" he went on scathingly. "Mountaired has a position at Court second to none except for the members of the Royal family."

He took a deep breath before he continued:

"He is immensely wealthy. He has a house in London besides one at Newmarket and a hunting-lodge in Leicestershire. Good God, girl, what more do you want?"

He glared at Salema as he spoke.

Bravely, because she was frightened of her Father when he shouted at her, she replied:

"I want to . . . marry somebody I . . . love!"

"Love!" the Earl said scathingly. "Do women think of nothing else? That, my dear girl, comes after marriage, and of course you will love the Duke when you are his wife, just as he will love you."

He did not wait for Salema to reply, but turned to his wife, saying:

"Surely you have enough sense, Elizabeth, to

realise that our daughter is an extremely fortunate young woman?"

"All the same, George, it is something of a shock," the Countess murmured.

"A shock?" the Earl repeated. "Of course it is! It was a shock when Swinton's horse pushed *Shining Star* and *Victorious* out of his way to pass the winning-post ahead of them."

He paused before he went on:

"It was a shock to find that the Duke and I were both listed second and that Swinton's horse won at sixteen to one."

There was silence for a moment.

He was remembering that was when he and the Duke had started talking to each other.

"We were discussing Salema's marriage, George," the Countess reminded him gently. "I am saying that of course it is a shock for her to find she is to marry a man to whom you have not spoken for the last six years!"

"That is all forgotten," the Earl said. "Now that we are to collaborate with our horses, nothing could be more favourable for the future than that Salema should wear the Mountaired diamonds. I am very proud, very proud of you indeed, my dear!"

He put a heavy hand on Salema's shoulder.

She turned away from him and walked to the window.

She stood looking out with unseeing eyes at the garden outside.

The sun was making a halo of gold round her head.

The Earl looked at her approvingly as she stood silhouetted against the window.

She had pulled off her jacket as they had come into the Study and she looked very young and very lovely.

The outline of her breasts beneath the white blouse was that of a Greek goddess.

Impatiently, because she was silent, the Earl walked to the table and poured himself another glass of champagne.

"I had expected," he said angrily, "that you would both have been delighted by my news. God knows, women are always unpredictable, but this is ridiculous!"

"As I have just said, George," the Countess replied, "it is not only a surprise, but also a shock!"

"Then the sooner you both get over it, the better!" the Earl roared. "We are dining at the Castle to-night and I shall expect Salema to look her best. I have certainly not had my money's-worth out of the gowns you bought her in London, but now is the moment to wear the best of them."

"We are dining at the Castle to-night?" the Countess repeated.

"That is what I have just said," her husband answered, "and you will both be ready to leave here at seven-thirty. There will be no question of your being late!"

"No, of course not, George," the Countess said.

She looked towards her daughter a little anxiously.

Salema had not spoken or moved from the window.

The Earl drew his gold watch out of his waist-coat pocket.

"Luncheon will be ready in a few minutes," he said, "and after luncheon, Salema, you and I will go and look at the mares. I am going to decide which one shall be served first by *Victorious*."

As he finished speaking, the Earl walked from the Study.

They heard his foot-steps going down the passage.

As the door shut behind him, Salema turned to run to her Mother.

She knelt down beside her chair.

In a voice that was little above a whisper, she said:

"I cannot . . . do it, Mama . . . you know I . . . cannot do it!"

"I am sure, my dearest, it will be better than you fear," the Countess said. "I know we have always thought the Duke to be rather a cruel man, but I have been sorry for him because his son was such a disappointment. I can understand his wanting to marry again."

"Why was his son a disappointment?" Salema asked.

"I suppose you were too young to remember him," the Countess said, "but he was a very handsome boy, and because he was an only child I think the Duke expected too much of him."

"Where is he now? Why do we never hear of him?" Salema asked.

"There was a row soon after your Father and the Duke started fighting over Monk's Wood."

"What was the row about?"

"It was because the Earl, when he came down from Oxford, would not go into the Household

Regiment in which the Duke had served and which he looked on as the right training for his son."

"And then what happened?" Salema enquired.

"Of course I am only repeating gossip," her Mother replied, "but apparently while the Earl said he was going to travel and see the world, the Duke flew into a rage and cut him off without a penny."

"That is just the sort of thing he would do!" Salema said. "Oh, Mama, how can I marry a man like that? Besides, I have no wish to be married."

There was a panicky note in her voice, and the Countess put her hand over hers.

"I know, my Darling, it is hard," she said, "but it means so much to your Father."

She gave a little sigh before she said:

"It has always upset me that this terrible animosity has existed between our two Estates. The Duchess was very kind to me when I first came here after I was married."

"Surely, she might have continued her friendship with you however much Papa and the Duke were fighting with each other?" Salema questioned.

Her Mother smiled sadly.

"You know, dearest, as well as I do that Papa would not have allowed me to speak to the Duchess if he was not speaking to the Duke, and I am sure Mary was in exactly the same position as I was."

"In other words, she was completely under her husband's thumb!" Salema said. "Which I should be, if I married him—a man old enough to be my Father!"

"But, Darling, you will be a Duchess!"

"I do not want to be a Duchess!" Salema

protested. "I want to marry someone young—someone I love and who likes the same things I do."

"I am sure you will have a great deal in common with the Duke. After all, his horses are magnificent!" the Countess said.

Salema rose from her knees.

She was intelligent enough to realise that, whatever she thought secretly, her Mother would be obliged to be on her husband's side.

He wanted this marriage, and she knew only too well it would be of tremendous benefit to him.

Her Mother would therefore press her into accepting meekly what had been arranged.

She had the feeling that whatever she said, no-one would listen.

If she really fought fervently against accepting the Duke, her Father would force her to obey him.

She could not help remembering how, when he went into one of his rages, he would slap her face or hit her sharply on the back of her head.

This had not happened this past year, since she had grown up.

But she knew only too well that when he was angry, the whole house trembled.

No-one had the courage to refuse anything he demanded of them.

'I cannot marry the Duke . . . I cannot!' she thought.

Then, as she heard her Father's foot-steps coming back down the passage, she knew that it would be quite useless to say so.

He was still in a very genial mood, saying as he opened the Study door:

"Luncheon is nearly ready and I am hungry. I had to leave Ascot early this morning and dinner last night was inedible!"

"I am longing to hear about what happened at Windsor Castle," the Countess said. "I do hope they made you comfortable."

"It was just what I expected," the Earl said. "Dull, boring, and the food was an insult!"

"Is it really true?" the Countess asked. "I heard that it was not as luxurious as it was in the days of the late King, but I thought perhaps the tales were exaggerated."

They had reached the Dining-Room, and the Earl sat down at the head of the table.

"All I can tell you is," he said, "that Mountaired was as disgusted as I was. Economy is one thing—but when it comes to cheese-paring where one's guests are concerned, I consider it an insult!"

He gave a short laugh before he said:

"The Earl of Dudley, who, as you know, is celebrated for his *sotto voce* grumbles, said quite loudly, so that the King must have heard:

" 'What a change, to be sure! Cold *pâtés* and hot champagne!' "

"Oh, George, did he really say that? How embarrassing!"

"It was difficult not to laugh," the Earl said, "but it was true, and the wine is very inferior to anything I drank when King George was on the throne!"

"Is this really true?" the Countess asked. "And can the Court really be as dull as everybody says it is?"

"All I can tell you is that it is worse," the Earl said. "Queen Adelaide is not only dull but dowdy, and her Ladies-in-Waiting wear their evening gowns almost up to their necks, which is very different from King George's order that a *décolletage* should be as low as possible!"

He laughed at his joke.

Because the servants were listening, the Countess said quickly:

"I feel we should give the King and Queen a chance to rearrange things their own way before one is too critical."

"I agree with your idea, Elizabeth," the Earl replied, "and all I can tell you is that I am glad to-night to have something decent to eat. At least my claret is drinkable."

Salema had not spoken since they had sat down at the table.

She was finding it impossible to eat.

She felt as though, when she least expected it, the ceiling had collapsed on her head.

Her whole world had turned topsy-turvy.

How could she have imagined in her wildest dreams that her father would make up his six-year-old row with the Duke and that their peace-making should involve her?

"I cannot . . . marry him . . . I cannot!"

She felt the words were being repeated over and over in her brain.

For the moment she could not think what she could do about it or how she could convince him that the Duke would in no way suit her as a husband.

'Perhaps if I talk to him alone,' she thought. 'I could make him understand.'

She knew, however, that he was enjoying himself.

He was describing over and over again with a great deal of repetition the discomforts at Windsor Castle.

"His Majesty is bored stiff by racing," he was saying, "and you mark my words, Elizabeth, he will cut the stables down to nothing."

"Surely he enjoys the races?" the Countess asked.

"He did not watch the horses when they were running," the Earl said. "I am told his grooms drank too much last night and there was no-one exerting any authority over them."

"It seems a great pity," the Countess remarked.

"A pity? Of course it is a pity!" her husband snapped. "And I can tell you one thing—I am not accepting an invitation to Windsor Castle again. I am quite certain that Mountaired will say the same."

There was a note of satisfaction in his voice as he spoke which made Salema shiver.

She knew her Father so well.

She could not help being aware that it gave him great pleasure to be able to talk about the Duke.

He was delighted to identify himself with him.

Every time he did so she felt it was another nail in her coffin.

It would be more and more difficult to persuade him that she must refuse the Duke's offer of marriage.

She had a sudden impulse to ask Charles to help her.

Perhaps he could think of some way by which she could persuade her Father that she could not marry a man who was so old, who also had such an unpleasant reputation.

"I must try to get away and see Charles," she told herself when luncheon was finished.

She soon realised, however, that that would be impossible.

Her Father wanted her to go with him immediately to look at the mares.

If they were to be serviced by *Victorious*, he must offer the Duke the best.

After he had seen the mares they went to the stables.

The Earl had a long talk with the Chief Groom about yesterday's race for the Gold Cup.

"Ye didn't stay for t'day's racing, M'Lord?"

The Earl shook his head.

"I decided that *Red Flag* did not have much of a chance," he replied, "and actually, we have a dinner-party to-night which is of more importance."

For one moment Salema thought he would tell the Head Groom where they were going.

As if he thought he had said enough, her Father moved down the stables to look at his horses.

He had not many.

But every one was a particularly finely-bred animal, and he enjoyed riding them all.

He kept his race-horses at Epsom.

It did not seem to worry him that his Manager would be extremely upset that *Shining Star* had been beaten in the race for the Gold Cup.

It was not difficult for Salema to understand that all her Father was thinking of at the moment was his future connection with the Duke.

They were going to the Castle to-night.

She could understand that he thought it was a triumph for him personally.

Actually, it was a triumph for common sense.

What she minded was that her Father was thinking nothing of her except that, as a Duchess, she would be of tremendous importance to the County.

As her Father, this would reflect on him.

For the first time in her life she realised that to him she was not a person with thoughts and feelings.

She was just something that belonged to him!

As they walked away from the stables, she thought now was her opportunity to tell her Father what she felt.

Yet, as the moved out of earshot of the grooms, he said:

"It is tea-time, and immediately after you have had your tea, I want you to go upstairs and rest. You must look your best to-night, and I shall be very disappointed if you do not do me proud."

"But, Papa, I want to . . . talk to you," Salema protested.

"There is no time for talking," the Earl said quickly. "You must lie down and rest, and mind you are not late! Mountaired is a stickler for punctuality, and we do not want to get off on the wrong foot."

"But . . . Papa . . . !"

"Now, do as I say," the Earl interrupted, "and stop looking as if you have lost half-a-crown and found a three-penny bit. You should be smiling and dancing for joy!"

"I want to feel like that, Papa . . . but . . ."

"No 'buts' and no arguments," the Earl snapped. "Now, come along, tea should be ready, and as soon as you have had a cup, upstairs to bed!"

There was nothing Salema could do but obey him.

Only when she was lying down did she think that Charles was waiting for her in Monk's Wood.

He would wait in vain.

'I suppose, after this, I shall never see him . . . again!' she thought.

Then she remembered his kiss, and the feelings it had aroused in her.

That was what she wanted when she married.

'Perhaps it is . . . something I shall . . . never feel . . . again,' she thought despairingly.

Although the sunshine was streaming through the window, the whole room felt dark.

* * *

Because there was nothing else she could do, Salema had her bath when it was brought to her bedroom.

Her Mother's lady's-maid had arranged her hair in the latest fashion, as she had worn it in London.

She put on the gown in which she had been presented.

It was the most expensive of all those they had bought.

Now it occurred to Salema that perhaps her Father and Mother thought it could also serve as her wedding-gown.

It had frill upon frill of chiffon round the hem of the full skirt.

A sash, embroidered with *diamanté*, encircled her tiny waist.

Diamanté was sprinkled on the puffed sleeves and round the neck of the gown.

It made her look very young, and, at the same time, almost as if she had stepped down from the sky.

She might have been one of the stars that glittered in the firmament.

"You look lovely, M'Lady!" the lady's-maid said as she buttoned her up the back.

It flashed through Salema's mind that she would like Charles to see her.

Then, because she was frightened of what lay ahead, she found herself crying out for him.

'I must . . . see him to-morrow . . . I *must!*' she thought. 'Perhaps I can . . . creep out before . . . Papa comes down to . . . breakfast and just . . . hope he will be . . . there.'

The maid placed her velvet wrap over her shoulders and opened the bedroom door.

As she went to the top of the stairs her father was waiting in the Hall.

"Come along! Come along!" he exclaimed. "I have no wish to be late, and, God knows, women are always unpunctual."

Salema was coming down the stairs and her Mother had already reached the bottom step.

The grandfather clock in the corner of the Hall showed that it was one minute to half-past seven.

The Earl, however, bustled them into the large carriage that was waiting outside.

It was drawn by two of his best horses.

A footman covered their knees with a fur rug.

Then he straightened his cockaded hat, which matched that of the coachman, before he jumped up on the box.

"Fortunately, we do not have far to go," the Earl

said. "I must admit I am eager to see what the Castle is like inside. I heard last year that Mountaired was making a number of improvements."

"I seem to remember you remarking at the time, George, that it was an unnecessary extravagance!" the Countess remarked.

"Nonsense!" the Earl retorted. "Improvements are always necessary if one is to have any respect for one's successors, and of course one's family."

Salema drew in her breath.

She knew that her Father was thinking of her children who would enjoy the improvements made to the Castle, the children she would have by an old man because he was disappointed in his son.

They passed through the village.

Two huge wrought-iron gold-tipped gates were flanked on either side by Lodges.

The horses passed through them.

Now they were moving up a long drive with ancient oak trees standing like sentinels on either side of it.

Salema had been to the Castle twice when she was a small girl, once, when there had been a Gymkhana which everybody in the County attended, and another time, just before the quarrel between her Father and the Duke, when she had been at a Meet.

It was one that took place annually.

Never again, after the trouble between the two Landlords, had she been permitted to go there.

She thought now she had forgotten how impressive the Castle was.

In its own way it was beautiful.

It dated back to Norman times.

But there was very little left of the original building except for one tower.

The rest of the house had been added later and was extremely impressive.

There were two wings on either side of a centre building on which was flying the Duke's standard.

There was a long flight of steps leading up to the front-door.

They had been covered with a red carpet.

She saw the smile on her Father's face.

She knew he was enjoying every minute of the 'burying of the hatchet.'

Salema only wished that she did not feel so nervous.

Her fingers were cold.

There was a heavy weight on her chest which made it hard to breathe.

Her Father stepped from the carriage first and helped her Mother alight.

As they walked up the steps, Salema followed them.

There seemed to be an enormous number of servants in the vast Hall.

It had a great carved oak staircase and a huge medieval fireplace.

A Butler went ahead to lead the way.

As two footmen threw open the double doors he announced in stentorian tones:

"The Earl and Countess of Ledgebourne, and Lady Lettice Bourne."

Salema saw a large room in which the tapers of three crystal chandeliers were lit.

Standing in front of the marble fireplace there was a man.

As he moved towards them she knew she could not look at him.

She stared down at the ground.

The pattern of the carpet was jumping up at her and making every step she took an effort.

Then she heard the Duke say:

"Good-evening, Ledgebourne. I am delighted to see you and, of course, Countess, I welcome you to the Castle!"

"We are so pleased to be here, Your Grace," Salema heard her Mother say in her soft, gentle voice.

"And this is Lettice!"

With a superhuman effort Salema managed to raise her head and look up at him.

He was taller than she had expected and also older.

His hair was white, his face lined.

He took her hand as she curtsied and she wanted to scream.

She could not . . . she would not . . . marry him!

"It is a very great pleasure to meet you, Lady Lettice," the Duke was saying. "Let me say that you are just as beautiful as I expected you to be."

His hand was still holding hers.

She thought his fingers were hard and there was no warmth in them.

She tried to reply, but the words would not come.

Then, as it was immaterial whether she spoke or not, the Duke said:

"Now I have a surprise for all of you, and it was also a surprise to me. My son is here to-night and I think you, Ledgebourne, will remember Stafford, although it is a long time since you have seen him."

The Duke, still holding Salema's hand, had drawn her forward as he spoke.

Now, without her being conscious of doing so, she looked towards the man of whom he was speaking.

Then, as she did so, she felt she must be dreaming and it could not be true.

It was Charles who stood there—Charles, looking incredibly smart in his evening clothes.

And he was looking at her with astonishment.

chapter four

DINNER was in what Salema was to learn was "the small Dining-Room."

They sat at a round table.

The Duke was in a carved chair that was almost like a throne.

He placed the Countess on his right and Salema on his left.

She thought for one moment she was going to have Charles sitting beside her.

Instead, just before dinner was announced, the Duke's Mother, who was very old and frail, came into the Dining-Room.

Salema had heard of her because she lived in the Dower House on her son's Estate.

However, she had never seen her.

She realised she was still beautiful.

At the same time, she walked with difficulty.

The Duke hurried to help her as she walked across the room.

Almost as soon as she had arrived, dinner was served.

The Dowager Duchess was supported on Charles's arm as she walked towards the Dining-Room.

The rest of the party followed casually, for, as the Duke said jovially:

"We are a family party and therefore there is no need for formality."

As he spoke he looked at Salema and she shuddered.

When they were seated round the table the conversation immediately turned to Ascot.

The running of the Duke and the Earl's horses and Lord Swinton's intervention were related in every detail.

Salema, however, found it hard to concentrate on what anybody was saying.

All she was conscious of was that Charles was there.

She felt as if her heart had suddenly come alive.

'Why did he not . . . tell me?' she asked.

Then she remembered the unpleasant things she had said about his Father.

Afterwards she could not recall what she ate or, for that matter, what she had said to the Duke.

He spoke to her once or twice, and she supposed she had answered him.

She could not help her eyes straying across the table towards Charles.

Once or twice he looked at her.

She felt he was telling her something she did not understand.

Course followed course.

Then Salema heard the Duke say to the Butler:

"Bring champagne for everyone."

The Butler looked surprised.

"I've served the port and the liqueurs, Your Grace."

"Do as I tell you!" the Duke ordered.

The man hurried away.

Salema thought it was just the way she expected the Duke to speak.

Again she was shivering and asking herself how she could possibly marry this old man.

She was sure he was just as cruel and unpleasant as she had always believed him to be.

How was it possible that Charles—Charles of all people—was his son?

The Butler came back with the champagne.

A fresh glass was set beside everyone and filled up.

The servants left the room and the Duke said:

"As I have already said, we are a family party and I think you all understand why you are here, and why this is a very special occasion."

The Earl was listening with a smile on his lips.

Salema, however, felt as if an icy hand were clutching her heart.

She knew what was to come.

She longed to prevent it but had no idea how she could do so.

The Duke continued:

"I think you all know that I have decided to marry again and have chosen as my wife the most beautiful woman in England!"

He paused and then continued:

"I therefore ask you to drink a toast to our happiness, and to my future close collaboration with my friend and neighbour, the Earl of Ledgebourne!"

He raised his glass slowly, as the others raised theirs.

The only exceptions were Salema and Charles.

She did not move and neither did he.

Their eyes met across the table and she thought he must see the agony in hers.

The Duke was obviously delighted with himself.

He went on to toast the success of servicing the Earl's mares with his stallion.

"To ensure," he said, "that within a few years, if not before, the Gold Cup will be ours."

The Earl then made a speech.

He was, he said, so glad and happy that the controversy between their two Estates was now at an end.

He thought the best thing they could do would be to divide Monk's Wood between them.

It was then that Salema gave a little cry.

"No, no!" she exclaimed.

The Duke turned to look at her.

"No?" he queried. "You do not like the idea?"

"Monk's Wood is special and sacred," Salema answered. "It is a sanctuary for the birds, and I am sure if you and Papa divide it, you will bring very bad luck."

"Bad luck?" the Duke repeated. "I cannot think why."

"As I have told you," Salema said, "it is a 'No-Man's-Land' and the villagers believe it is haunted by the ghost of the Monk who built the Chapel there."

The Duke laughed.

"The villagers believe anything that suits them!" he said. "Personally, I do not believe in ghosts or any of that sort of nonsense, and the sooner Monk's Wood is cleared of its vermin, the better!"

Again Salema gave a cry.

"Please," she begged, "please . . . do not do anything so . . . wrong and so . . . cruel! Monk's Wood is a very special place. I could not bear it to be spoilt."

The Duke hesitated.

She knew he was wondering whether he should tell her to shut up and not make a nuisance of herself.

Then unexpectedly he succumbed.

"Very well," he said, "you shall have my half of Monk's Wood as a wedding present and your Father can give you the other half. Does that satisfy you?"

It was with the greatest difficulty that Salema forced herself to say "thank you."

But it was a wedding present that made her feel as if it were another bar of the prison into which she was being forced, a prison from which there was no escape.

She had the strange idea that Charles understood exactly what she was feeling.

She looked at him in despair.

There was an expression in his eyes which made her want to plead with him to help her.

There was more champagne and more toasts, until finally the Dowager Duchess said weakly:

"I think the Ladies should withdraw. I must go home as I am very tired."

"Of course, Mama," the Duke said. "It was very kind of you to come, and I wanted you to be here on such an auspicious occasion."

"Of course, I understand," the Dowager Duchess agreed.

Charles helped her to her feet.

She leaned on his arm as they walked towards the door.

"See your grandmother off, Stafford," the Duke shouted. "Then come back."

As he spoke his son's Christian name, Salema remembered she had heard it before.

When he had called himself 'Charles,' it had never occurred to her for one moment that he might belong to the Aired family.

Now she could understand why he was riding on the Duke's Estate when Rufus had fallen into one of the treacherous man-traps.

She followed her Mother out of the Dining-Room.

Once in the corridor, they had to go slowly because the Dowager Duchess and Charles were just ahead of them.

They reached the Hall.

A footman hurried to collect a fur cape which was lying on a chair.

It belonged to the Dowager Duchess.

Without really thinking of a reason for doing so, Salema took it from him.

She put it round the Dowager Duchess's shoulders.

"Thank you, dear," the Duchess murmured.

Another footman opened the front-door.

Still holding on to Charles with one hand, the Dowager Duchess put her other on Salema's arm.

Slowly they moved down the steps.

It was an effort for the elderly woman, and Charles actually lifted her into the carriage that was waiting at the foot of them.

The footman shut the door and sprang onto the box.

The horses moved off.

The Dowager Duchess leant forward to wave to them.

It was then Salema was aware that she and Charles were alone together at the bottom of the steps.

Without moving, he said in a low voice:

"I have to see you."

"I could not . . . come this . . . afternoon," Salema whispered.

"I waited," he replied, "because I have a lot to tell you. Meet me to-night in Monk's Wood."

"In Monk's Wood?" Salema exclaimed.

"I will wait there until dawn if necessary, but I must see you."

"Yes . . . of course."

Charles turned and climbed back up the steps.

Salema was forced to do the same.

When they reached the Hall there were two footmen in attendance.

Charles merely said:

"Your Mother will be in the Drawing-Room."

He walked away down the corridor.

Salema went into the Drawing-Room.

Her Mother was seated in an armchair, and she walked slowly towards her.

The Countess looked at her anxiously.

"I cannot understand," she said at length, "why His Grace did not speak to you privately, Dearest, before he announced his intention of marrying you."

"I cannot . . . marry him . . . Mama! You . . . know I cannot!" Salema answered.

The Countess did not speak.

Salema knew she was thinking that the die was cast and there was nothing she or anyone else could do about it now.

She found it impossible to put what she was feeling into words or make her Mother understand.

She walked to the window and looked out over the garden.

It was beautifully kept, the flower-beds bright with colour.

She knew that the Duke employed a great number of gardeners, while her Father could afford only two.

The Castle was magnificent—she had to admit that.

The description of its contents, of which she had heard so much, was not exaggerated.

And yet she was thinking that for her the whole place would seem like a funeral vault if she lived there with the Duke.

Then, almost like a light coming from Heaven, she remembered that within a few hours she would be with Charles.

Although it seemed impossible, Charles might save her.

He had saved Rufus, so why not her?

Yet, if all the stories and gossip were to be believed, Charles was in his Father's "Black Books."

It was therefore strange to find him at the Castle to-night.

'I do not understand,' Salema thought.

Yet, because he was there she was not so terrified

as she had been earlier in the evening.

When the Gentlemen joined the Ladies, the Duke and the Earl were laughing.

Salema thought she had never seen her Father in such good spirits.

She knew the reason and could hardly bear to express it even to herself.

Now the Countess rose, saying:

"I am sure, Your Grace, you will forgive us if we go home early, but my husband only arrived back from Ascot to-day, and although he will not admit it, he is very tired. It is a long drive, as you well know."

"I am also somewhat tired," the Duke said, "but so elated by our plans for the future that I feel I have no wish for this happy evening to end."

"That is what it has been," the Earl agreed, "a very happy evening, and do not forget, Your Grace, you are lunching with us to-morrow, after which we will inspect the mares."

"We will certainly do that," the Duke said, "and of course I have a great deal to say to my beautiful new wife-to-be."

He turned towards Salema as he spoke and took her left hand in his.

"To-morrow," he said, "I will bring you a ring which will grace your third finger and with which I feel sure you will be delighted."

It was as he touched her that Salema felt she was being menaced by a reptile.

She felt every nerve in her body shiver.

It was with the greatest difficulty that she did not snatch her hand from his.

As the Countess moved towards the door the

Duke raised Salema's hand.

She felt his lips against her skin.

Suddenly she knew she would rather die than marry him. Nothing or nobody could force her to become his wife.

She was, however, saved from saying anything by her Father.

He put a heavy hand on the Duke's shoulder.

"We have a great many things to decide to-morrow," he said. "Thank you for this evening. It has certainly been a compensation for losing the Ascot Gold Cup!"

He laughed as if at a joke, and the Duke said:

"It is only a question of time, Ledgebourne, before we not only have the Gold Cup in our grasp, but youngsters to ride the horses we breed!"

He put his arm round Salema's shoulders as he spoke.

She knew by his expression exactly to what he was referring.

She felt her repulsion sweep through her like a tidal wave.

It was with the greatest difficulty that she prevented herself from screaming that she would never bear his children.

The Earl was moving towards the door.

Salema would have followed him, but the Duke held her back.

"You are very beautiful, my dear," he said in a thick voice, "and to-morrow I will tell you more eloquently than I can at this moment what I think about you."

His eyes were on her lips.

Because she could no longer control her feelings, she shook herself free of him and ran after her Father.

She reached the Hall.

A footman put her velvet evening coat over her shoulders and she ran down the steps.

She reached the carriage where her Mother was waiting.

Looking back, Salema realised her Father was still laughing and talking with the Duke.

It was some minutes before he came to join them.

As they drove away from the Castle he said with satisfaction:

"That was tremendous! I can hardly believe I am not dreaming!"

"It is certainly something I did not expect to happen," the Countess said. "It is years since we were last inside the Castle."

"All that is forgotten," the Earl replied, "and the Duke is eager for the marriage to take place as quickly as possible."

Salema drew in her breath.

She was just about to say that it was something that would never happen.

Then she told herself it would be a mistake until she had talked to Charles.

She must find out from him what he thought before she ran away.

If that was not possible, she would throw herself off the top of the house.

'I will not . . . marry the Duke . . . I will . . . not!' she thought hysterically.

She pressed her lips together to prevent herself from saying it aloud.

They arrived back at the house.

The Earl gave instructions on the last part of the drive as to what they should have for luncheon the following day.

He also kept saying over and over again how much he had enjoyed dinner at the Castle.

When the horses came to a standstill, Salema jumped out.

She ran up the stairs without saying good-night.

"What the devil is the matter with Salema?" the Earl asked his wife.

"I should leave her alone, Dear," the Countess replied. "She is finding it hard to get used to marrying anyone, let alone the Duke, who, until yesterday was, if you remember, your most hated enemy."

"Enemy?" the Earl repeated. "Nonsense! We had an argument over Monk's Wood and the less that is said about that in the future, the better! After all, you heard him give half of it to Salema as a wedding-present and I will give her the rest. What more can the girl want?"

The Countess did not reply.

Having reached the Hall, she merely climbed slowly up the stairs.

If her husband felt jubilant, she was in fact very tired.

She contemplated going in to say good-night to Salema, but thought it would be a mistake.

Instead, she went into her own bedroom where her lady's-maid was waiting.

*   *   *

Salema's maid was not in her bedroom and she did not ring for her.

Instead, she changed quickly, putting on her riding-habit.

She waited until she heard her Father come up to bed.

She slipped out of her room and down the back stairs, which took her to the door nearest to the stables.

The servants, except for those on duty in the Hall, had all retired early.

There was no-one to observe her as she let herself out.

She hurried through the bushes and down the path to the stables.

Because the Earl economised, he did not have a groom on duty at night.

"No-one is likely to try to steal my horses," he said proudly. "They respect me in the neighbourhood, and most of the men have won a few pounds backing them."

"Of course, Dear," the Countess agreed.

She had also agreed to their saving on extra footmen by not having one on duty in the Hall at night.

It was not difficult for Salema to saddle *Flash*.

She had done it so often before.

She led him to the mounting-block and climbed into the saddle.

She rode off, leaving the stable by the far end.

It was impossible from there to be seen from the house.

As she did so, she thought that only Charles could think of her meeting him in Monk's Wood in the middle of the night.

It was an adventure in itself.

She had never before crept out of the house after she was supposed to have gone to bed.

She had certainly also never met a young man unchaperoned, in the moonlight.

She rode *Flash* across the flat fields, then entered the Wood.

The birds that were asleep in the boughs rose in protest at her intrusion.

There was also a good deal of rustling in the undergrowth as *Flash* moved down the mossy path.

There was no need to guide him—he knew the way as well as she did.

She arrived at the pond in Monk's Wood.

For one moment she was dismayed to find that Charles was not there.

Then, as he came from the shadows, she slid down from *Flash*'s back.

Without thinking, without considering, she ran towards him.

She flung herself against him, and his arms went round her.

Then he was kissing her, kissing her passionately, demandingly, possessively, as if he made her his and there was no need for words.

Only when they were both breathless did she say:

"Oh, Charles . . . what am I . . . to do? What can . . . I do?"

He put his arm round her and drew her towards the fallen tree where they had sat before.

"I have a lot to tell you, my Darling," he said.

"Charles . . . I am . . . desperate! Completely and . . . absolutely desperate! I could not . . . believe it was . . . true when my Father came . . . back from. . . Ascot."

She felt Charles' arm tighten round her.

They looked at each other for a long moment before she said:

"Why did you not . . . tell me . . . who you were?"

"For the same reasons," Charles said in a deep voice, "that you did not tell me who you were. I had no idea—I never guessed for a second that you might be the daughter of my Father's avowed enemy."

"How can . . . you be his . . . son?" Salema asked piteously.

"That is something I have often asked myself," Charles said grimly, "and now, my precious, I will tell you what you want to know. Shall we start at the beginning?"

Salema looked up at him.

The moon was full overhead, and she thought that no-one could look more handsome or attractive.

He was still wearing his evening clothes.

Because there was no horse to be seen, she knew he must have walked to Monk's Wood from the Castle.

If she was looking up at him, he was looking down at her.

Her hair looked silver instead of gold in the moonlight.

Her eyes seemed to fill her small, pointed face.

She did not seem to be human.

As he had thought when he had first seen her, there was something ethereal, spiritual, and Divine about her.

He thought she was not only a part of the

moonlight, but also of the Woods.

For one moment they just looked at each other.

Then when she thought Charles would kiss her again, he turned his head away.

"I have to make you understand," he said, "and do not tempt me into forgetting everything with your beauty or the irresistible sweetness of your lips."

When he spoke like that, Salema felt her heart move towards him.

She knew it was impossible not to love him.

He was the only person that mattered in her life.

"I am . . . listening," she said softly.

"I expect you have heard often enough how my Father and I had a furious row and I left home?"

"Yes . . . I have heard about it," Salema replied. "For a long time nobody talked about anything else. And when you vanished, there were many tales which nobody could substantiate, that you were exploring the world."

"Everything is true," Charles said, "but long before that happened, I found my Father intolerable to live with."

He gave a sigh before he continued:

"Because I was an only son, he was determined I should be a credit to him. I was bullied and pressured almost from the moment I left the cradle."

"In what way?" Salema questioned.

"In every way," Charles said. "I could not have lessons like ordinary boys of my age. I had to have special Tutors on every subject. If I did not get a favourable report from every one of them, there was Hell to pay!"

He sighed again as he said:

"He bullied and beat me, until I enjoyed School because I was away from him."

"Oh, Charles . . . how awful!" Salema said. "I cannot bear to think of you . . . unhappy."

"I was not only unhappy, I was abused!" Charles said. "After I had been to Oxford and known a great deal of freedom, I knew I could not go on being treated like a raw recruit."

"So you ran away."

"I ran away after my Father decided that I had to go into the family Regiment. I knew I would be taking orders in the same way that he had given them."

"I can . . . understand that," Salema said.

"I expect you know what happened after that," Charles said. "I told my Father I was going round the world and he said that if I did he would cut me off without a shilling."

"So it was . . . true!" Salema explained. "I have often wondered if that story was not . . . exaggerated."

"There was no exaggeration about it," Charles said. "It was an ultimatum. Either I could lose my freedom, or live as I intended to do."

"It was brave of you . . . very brave to . . . run away."

"I was fortunate in that my Grandmother, whom I have always loved and who loves me, understood my feelings," Charles went on.

"And she helped you."

"She gave me what money she could afford," Charles said. "It was not very much, but enough to keep me from starving. When I had spent what she allowed me for the year, I had to work in sometimes very unpleasant ways, but at least I was my own master, and I was not forced to do anything I did not want to do."

The way he spoke told Salema how much it had galled him to be at the beck and call of his Father.

He had a strong personality of his own.

She could understand how humiliating it had been for him not to express his own opinions and decide his own life.

"So you . . . saw the . . . world!" she said softly.

"A great deal of it," Charles admitted, "from the Himalayas to the African desert—from the Greek islands and the Pyramids to the Temples of Java. It was all a delight and very interesting."

Salema sighed.

"You are lucky . . . very lucky. It is what I have . . . longed to do . . . myself."

"There is so much I would like to show you," Charles said.

"To see such places with you would be like . . . entering through the . . . Gates of Heaven!" she murmured.

To her surprise, he took his arm from around her waist.

"Now, listen to me," he said, "for it is important for you to understand."

"You . . . know I am . . . listening," she answered.

"On my travels," he said, "of course I have found women—women of all nationalities from many different countries."

Salema looked at him in surprise.

It was not what she had expected him to say.

"You mean . . . you mean," she asked hesitatingly

after a moment, "you have . . . been in love?"

Charles smiled.

"I have been amused, attracted, and sometimes even a little infatuated, but never—and this is the truth—have I been in love—until I met you!"

"Oh . . . Charles . . . !"

"It is true," he said. "I swear it is true! And from the moment I saw you I knew you were everything I had sought for, everything I imagined a perfect woman should be."

"H-how could you have . . . known that?"

"I knew it instinctively," he said, "and I think, my Darling, when I kissed you that you felt the same about me."

"I . . . I felt I was a . . . part of you," Salema whispered.

"And that is what you are."

"B-but . . . what can I do . . . what can I do?" Salema cried.

Charles looked away from her before he said:

"First, let me tell you why I have come home. I received a letter from my Grandmother, who has corresponded with me the whole time I have been away, saying she was growing old and wished to see me once more before she died."

He paused and then continued:

"Because I love her and was indebted to her for what I was doing, there was nothing else I could do but come home as quickly as possible."

"So you . . . went to her . . . house."

"I had no intention of seeing my Father or having any further contact with him," Charles replied. "I knew only too well how he would abuse me."

"What . . . happened?"

87

"Yesterday, when I was sitting with my Grandmother, he walked in on his way back from the Ascot Races."

"He must . . . have been . . . surprised to . . . see you!"

"I expected him to bawl me out as he has done so often before and rage at me in an uncontrolled manner I always thought was vulgar, simply because I would not obey him."

"But . . . he did . . . not do . . . that!"

"No. He greeted me and said he had solved the problem of the differences between us."

He paused and then continued:

"He had come to see his Mother to tell her that he intended to be married again."

"It must have come as a surprise!" Salema said.

"As it happens," Charles answered, "I had never thought of him marrying again. I knew my Mother had died, of course, because my Grandmother told me about it. I was sorry I had not been there to say good-bye to her."

He sighed.

"But she had never been strong enough to support me against my Father, and it was my Grandmother who meant most to me and who I felt loved me just for myself."

"I thought to-night that she was . . . very beautiful," Salema said.

"To me she has always been a very wonderful person," Charles said, "and, as I told her, I could not have resisted all these years without her help and also without her encouragement."

"She encouraged you to stay away?" Salema asked.

"She warned me that it would be a mistake for me to come home with my Father still very bitter because I had not done as I was told."

"How can he . . . be so . . . stubborn?" Salema asked.

Charles gave a laugh that had no humor in it.

"You do not know my Father. He has no heart and no interest in anything that does not concern himself."

"I have always . . . thought him . . . very cruel," Salema said. "The way he has treated the villagers is horrible, and the man-traps, like the one from which you rescued Rufus which he has put all over his Estate, are lethal."

"It is something I always loathed him doing," Charles said. "It was another controversy over which we could never see eye-to-eye."

"I am glad you . . . felt like . . . that," Salema said.

She put out her hand towards him, but he did not take it.

"I have not finished yet," he said.

Salema waited.

"I told you that I love you," Charles answered. "When I met you yesterday I knew I could not go back to my wanderings over the world and leave you behind."

"Y-you . . . intended to ask . . . me to go . . . with you?" Salema said with a little cry.

"I could hardly believe, seeing how beautiful you are, that you would accept," Charles said, "but when you told me that it did not matter to you whether you lived in a Castle or a cave as long as you loved someone, I hoped and prayed that you loved me like that."

"As I . . . do!" Salema said in a whisper.

There was silence.

Then Charles said:

"I was thinking of you, waiting for you, and loving you all day."

"I could not get away from Papa," Salema said, "and he was so excited about coming to the Castle to-night."

"Just as my Father was excited when he came to my Grandmother's house to tell her he was to be married. He said he had plenty of time to have half-a-dozen other sons to take my place, as I had been such a failure to him."

"And what did you feel?" Salema asked.

"I do not care, one way or the other," Charles replied. "When my Grandmother dies she will leave me the same money I have been having these past six years and a few personal things. I was thinking that perhaps you and I could manage on that. But I shall have to find work of some sort or another so that we can keep our heads above water."

"Oh, Charles . . . that is . . . what I would love . . . and it would make me more happy than I can . . . possibly tell you."

Charles did not turn towards her.

As she looked at him in perplexity he said:

"I told you things had changed."

"You mean . . . you no longer . . . love me?"

"I love you as I have never loved anyone before," Charles said, "but now, if you marry my Father, you realise what lies ahead of you?"

Salema did not speak, and he went on:

"You will be a Duchess, you will be extremely rich, you will entertain in London anyone in whom you are interested. You can fill the Castle and my Father's other houses with amusing and intelligent people."

His voice was sharp as he finished speaking.

Salema moved a little closer to him as she said:

"Do you think . . . that is . . . what I . . . want?"

"Of course it is what you want!" he answered. "It is what any woman would want, and because you are so beautiful, you will be acclaimed at Buckingham Palace and anywhere else you set your foot."

He did not wait for her to speak, but went on:

"What can I offer you? A cave in the mountains which we have talked of before, a tent in the desert? Perhaps nothing but the moonlight in a Wood like this."

He voice deepened.

"Who will there be then to admire you, except for the wild animals, the birds, and perhaps—me!"

Salema laughed.

It was a very soft, gentle little laugh.

The she said:

"Oh, Charles, Darling, I thought we understood each other, and if we do, you know exactly what I am thinking. Do you imagine I would want any of those things without you? I love you . . . I love you!"

Charles turned round.

"Do you know what you are saying?" he asked.

"I know exactly what I am saying," Salema replied, "and a cave in the desert would be Paradise if you were with me, while the Castle, as I thought to-night, would be nothing but a prison in which I would be utterly and completely miserable."

Charles stared at her.

Then, surprisingly, he rose to his feet.

He pulled her to him and into his arms.

Then he kissed her.

It was not the wild, demanding kisses he had given her before.

His lips were soft and gentle, as if she were infinitely precious.

He raised his head to look down at her. He thought the moonlight was shining from within her.

She had a radiance that made her unhuman and somehow a part of the gods.

"I love you! Salema, I love and worship you!" he said. "But—are you sure?"

"Completely and absolutely sure," Salema whispered. "Oh, please, Charles . . . I cannot live . . . without you, and if you . . . leave me, all I will want to do is to . . . die!"

"Then we will be married," he said. "You may perhaps regret what you have given up for me, but you will live, my Darling, and that is all that matters."

Then he was kissing her again.

Now it was possessively, as if he made her his and there was no dividing them.

chapter five

A LONG while later Charles said:

"I must send you home, my Darling. You must sleep and I must plan what we are going to do."

Salema quivered against him.

"What . . . are we going . . . to do?" she whispered.

"We are going to be married," he answered, "and that is the first hurdle. After that we may have to struggle, but at least you will be mine."

"That is . . . all I want," Salema said, "but your Father will be very, very angry . . . and so will Papa."

"My Father has always been angry with me!" Charles said. "And it really does not worry me. I am just wondering how we can get married without any difficulties and where we can go and hide, at least for a little while before we go abroad."

Salema thought, then she gave a little cry.

"I know where we can go!" she exclaimed.

"Where?" Charles asked.

"To my old Nanny," she answered. "She has a cottage not far from here, but not on Papa's land, or your Father's."

"Do you think we can trust her?" Charles asked.

Salema laughed.

"With our lives and everything else. Nanny loves me and she always stood up for me when Papa was in one of his rages. She retired only three years ago."

"And you think that will be safe?" Charles said. "I really do not want us to start our honeymoon with both of our Fathers screaming abuse at us!"

He was making a joke of it, but Salema shivered.

"I am terrified when Papa is in one of his rages."

"I feel rather the same when my Father 'blows his top,'" Charles said, "and that was one of the reasons why I ran away."

"At least we will not be there to hear their anger," Salema said.

"Now, tell me where your Nanny lives and the Church that is nearest to it."

"Nanny lives in the village of Fladbury," Salema told him. "The Church is a very ancient one and the Rector is a charming old man who is rather blind."

"That sounds exactly what we want," Charles remarked.

He kissed her forehead before he said:

"First thing to-morrow I will go to London and get a Special Licence, and to make sure that nobody recognises me, I shall merely call myself 'Charles Aired.'"

"I cannot be married as Salema because I was christened Lettice Alverline Harriet Muriel."

Charles laughed.

"What a mouthful!"

"They were all my Godparents, and Mama wanted to call me Salema, but Papa said it was a Hebrew name, so he would not allow it."

"It is what I shall always call you," Charles said. "But I am afraid, Darling, you will have to be married as 'Harriet.' It sounds very respectable and I am sure no one will recognise you with such a pompous name."

"I doubt if the Rector of Fladbury would be suspicious of anyone!" Salema said. "I have often sat at the back of the Church with Nanny and thought he conducted the Service beautifully, but I have never actually met him."

"Just leave the Rector to me," Charles said. "But will you tell your Nanny?"

"I will go over there to-morrow," Salema agreed, "and let her know exactly what we are doing. I know she will fight for us and defend us against our parents."

"In future I will fight for you," Charles said. "I promise you, my Darling, I shall be very protective and also very jealous."

Salema laughed.

"There will be no need for that. If there are other men in the world except you, I shall not even see them."

"I will make sure of that," Charles said firmly, "but unfortunately *they* will see *you*."

He kissed Salema again.

She clung to him, feeling that the moonlight enveloped them with a light that could only have come from God.

As if he forced himself to be sensible, Charles

took her to *Flash*, who was standing by the pool.

He lifted her into the saddle.

"Take care of yourself, my lovely one," he said. "You know we cannot meet to-morrow, as I shall be in London, but I will be waiting here early on Saturday morning."

Salema thought quickly.

"Papa usually has breakfast at half-past-eight," she said. "If I leave the house at seven, no-one will ask questions about where I am going."

"Then I will be here at seven," Charles said, "and we can make all our plans to run away as quickly as possible."

She knew he was thinking that he did not want her to be upset or frightened by his Father more than was necessary.

She reached out her hand to him.

"I love . . . you!" she said.

He kissed her fingers one by one, then he said:

"God go with you, and may you come to no harm before we are together again."

She smiled at him before she urged *Flash* forward.

He watched her until she was out of sight.

Then, turning towards the Castle, he walked quickly back the way he had come.

The Duke had insisted quite unnecessarily, Charles thought, that he should stay the night.

But he was determined to leave early in the morning.

What he needed was two fast horses and a light travelling carriage to get him to London as quickly as possible.

He had no compunction about taking them from his Father's stables.

He knew the Duke had been delighted when he had found him at his Grandmother's house.

It had given him great pleasure to humiliate him with the news that he was going to marry again.

It was also this which made him insist that he should stay at the Castle.

He hoped this would make him realise how much he could lose by not being a dutiful son.

Charles let himself in by the garden door through which he had left the Castle.

He went up the stairs to his bedroom.

That again was a deliberate attempt by his Father to make him aware of his stupidity in preferring discomfort.

He guessed what his son must have endured on his travels and meant to impress on him the luxuries he had lost.

Charles was therefore sleeping in one of the State Rooms in a huge four-poster bed.

There were some extremely fine pictures on the walls.

As a young man he had been on the Second Floor.

He suspected his room there would be exactly the same as when he had left it.

Before he went away he had taken his clothes and some of his very special treasures to his Grandmother's house.

She had, as she had promised, kept them safe until his return.

He found it extraordinary that, having been away so long, his clothes still fitted him as comfortably as they had six years ago.

He knew that while his muscles had developed, he had been forced to live frugally.

He had also taken an enormous amount of exercise.

Because of that, he had not put on extra weight, as is customary when a man gets older, but had lost it.

He undressed.

He made a mental note to tell the servants in the morning to take his evening clothes back to the Dower House.

He thought it would be wise for Salema to leave her more expensive gowns there when they went abroad.

He was sensible enough to realise that it would be difficult to buy winter clothes such as furs and heavy coats on the very little money they would have.

Now that Salema was not with him, he wondered if he was not asking too much.

How could he expect any woman to share with him the privations and discomforts which had been inevitable during his travels?

Then he told himself that Salema was different.

He could not imagine any woman he had met refusing without a qualm the position of a Duchess and the great wealth that went with it.

He knew that Salema had been absolutely truthful in saying that all she wanted was his love.

He went to the window and looked up at the moon.

'How can I have been so fortunate,' he asked, 'to have found somebody who is so different, so perfect in every way?'

He said a prayer of thankfulness as he got into the huge canopied bed.

It was as comfortable as sleeping on a cloud, and the linen was the finest available.

But all he could think of was that very shortly he would hold Salema in his arms.

Once she was his, he would never lose her.

* * *

The following day passed very slowly.

It was difficult for Salema to concentrate on anything that was being said or done.

Her Father was fussing over the luncheon and waiting impatiently for the Duke to arrive.

They rode a little way over the fields, but all he was concerned with was that the Duke should be impressed by what he saw, also that His Grace should not feel he was being condescending in marrying Lettice.

"I may not be wealthy," the Earl was saying, "but my lineage is just as good as Mountaired's. In fact I was thinking last night that he has a number of blots on his escutcheon, while I have very few."

"Does it really matter to-day what happened yesterday," Salema asked as he paused for breath.

"It matters to somebody as important as Mountaired," the Earl replied, "and I can assure you, my dear, that beautiful though you are, if you were the daughter of an unknown Country Squire, he would not have asked you to be his wife."

Salema wanted to say that his son had loved her when he did not know who she was.

Instead, she merely said:

"I hope, Papa, you will not be disappointed when

you know the Duke better."

"Disappointed? Why should I be disappointed?" the Earl asked sharply.

"Can you have forgotten so quickly all the things you have said about him?" Salema enquired. "And also those that have been said by other people?"

The Earl urged his horse forward.

"I do not know what you are talking about!" he replied.

* * *

The Duke arrived in time for luncheon in a very smart Phaeton drawn by horses which he knew would impress the Earl.

Salema thought, as he walked into the house, that he looked slightly contemptuous.

It was so much smaller than his own.

He drank champagne before luncheon and a great deal of the excellent claret that was served with the meal.

The Earl had given instructions about the servants' uniforms. They were to be immaculate.

The silver should have a higher polish than usual.

The flowers that decorated the table were to be the very best from the greenhouses.

Salema was quite certain that all this was wasted on the Duke, but she did not say so.

When the coffee had been served and the Duke had accepted a glass of brandy, the servants withdrew.

"Now that we are alone," the Earl said, "I am wondering, Your Grace, if you have decided exactly when your marriage to Salema should take place?"

"I thought in three weeks' time," the Duke replied.

"Is that not rather soon?" the Countess asked.

"It is not soon enough for me!" the Duke replied. "But we have to have the Banns called, and of course give our friends time to accept your invitation to the wedding, and to send us, we hope, some decent presents!"

"That brings us to about the fifth of July," the Earl said, "and I think the sixth, which is a Saturday, would be an excellent day. Besides our London friends, all the County will wish to come, and of course we must provide a marquee for both the tenants and employees on our Estates."

"That is exactly what I was thinking," the Duke agreed, "and perhaps you will insert the announcement of the engagement in *The London Gazette* immediately."

"Of course, of course," the Earl said, beaming at the idea.

Salema clenched her fingers together in her lap.

She thought if she sat quietly and said nothing, no-one would notice her.

It was only after they left the Dining-Room and went into the Drawing-Room that the Earl said:

"Now, Your Grace, I want to show you my mares."

"I am looking forward to seeing them," the Duke answered, "but first I have something for your daughter, and I think perhaps it would be best if we could be alone."

"You can go into my Study," the Earl said. "Nobody will disturb you there."

Salema was terrified.

She was sure the Duke not only intended to give her the engagement ring as he had promised, but would also try to kiss her.

Quickly, stammering a little because she was frightened, she said to the Duke:

"I . . . I k-know . . . because y-you said so . . . that you h-have the engagement ring with you . . . p-please . . . give it to me here . . . so that Papa and Mama can see it."

The Duke raised his eye-brows.

But, because he wanted to show off the ring he had brought with him, he agreed.

He produced a small leather box from his pocket and opened it.

It contained a large heart-shaped diamond surrounded by smaller stones.

It was a 16th-century piece of jewellery which was extremely valuable.

The Duke could not resist telling the Earl, who was looking at it appreciatively, how long it had been in his family.

"And now, of course, I must put it on my Bride-to-Be's finger," he said.

He reached for Salema's left hand as he spoke and pressed the huge diamond onto her third finger.

Once again, because he was touching her, Salema felt revolted.

At the same time, she felt a streak of fear run through her.

Supposing she was never able to return the ring and could never escape from the Duke?

Then she thought of Charles.

She felt she could see him smiling at her reassuringly.

Quickly she took her hand from the Duke's, saying:

"Thank you . . . thank you very much . . . it is a very . . . beautiful ring."

"I knew you would admire it," the Duke said complacently, "and there are a great many other diamonds to go with it which will make you even more beautiful than you are at this moment. The tiara which you will wear at your wedding and of course at the Opening of Parliament is larger than that of any other Peeress."

"I suppose," the Earl said eagerly, "that Lettice will also be a hereditary Lady of the Bedchamber."

"Of course," the Duke agreed, "and I know Queen Adelaide will be very delighted and indeed fortunate to have her."

"I only hope she will not have to spend too long at Court," the Earl remarked. "I have not forgotten the boredom we had to endure the other night!"

"I shall want Lettice with me," the Duke said firmly, "and she will have little time for other duties."

As he spoke he looked at Salema in a way which made her take a step backwards.

Then, because she was frightened that he still might want to see her alone, she said:

"Now it is your turn, Papa, to take His Grace to see the mares. I hope that he thinks them worthy of his magnificent stallion."

"Come along, come along!" the Earl said delightedly, and walked towards the Drawing-Room door.

As soon as the Duke had passed through it, Salema pulled the diamond ring from her finger.

Because she was frightened, she felt the light in it was like an eye which regarded her evilly.

"It is a beautiful ring," her Mother was saying.

"I wonder if the other women who have worn it have been happy?" Salema asked.

"I am sure they were," the Countess answered quickly.

"Not if their husbands were all like the present Duke!" Salema replied.

"Now, Darling, you have to be sensible about this," her Mother said, "and allow your Father to know what is best for you. You are very young and have not met many men. I am sure the Duke is already very much in love with you."

"He is in love with the idea of having more sons! I cannot believe that they, or anyone else, will be able to change his character or his behaviour," Salema said hotly, "however much Papa tried to forget it!"

The Countess sighed.

"I only hope that you will not say such things to your Father. It will only upset him, and you know as well as I do that he has set his heart on this marriage."

Salema knew there was no point in arguing.

She merely walked towards the door.

"Surely, you are going with your Father and the Duke?" the Countess enquired as she reached it.

"When His Grace returns," Salema answered, "will you tell him, Mama, that I have a headache and am lying down? So I will be unable to say good-bye to him."

Salema went from the room before her Mother could answer.

Instead of going upstairs, she ran out into the garden.

She entered the shrubbery where she had hidden as a child from her Nurses and Governess.

They had always been unable to find her.

She went there now and, sitting down under the trees, she thought about Charles.

She felt as if her thoughts winged towards him like birds.

Wherever he was he must know she was thinking of him and loving him.

"I love you! I love you!" she murmured beneath her breath.

Then she looked up to see above her head a white dove regarding her with his head on one side.

Because it was the bird of Aphrodite, the Goddess of Love, she felt it was an omen of Good Luck.

'I shall need all the luck in the world,' she thought, 'and it is what I shall have if I am able to marry Charles!'

When Salema came down for dinner the Earl was in a rage.

"What the devil do you think you are playing at?" he asked furiously. "Mountaired thought it extraordinary that you just disappeared and your Mother said you were lying down. Young women never lie down in the afternoon!"

"I wanted to rest . . . and think," Salema said meekly.

"Think? What have you got to think about? I do all the thinking around here! All you and your Mother have got to do is to make a list of those we intend to invite to the wedding and you can start to address the envelopes!"

Salema did not answer, and her Father grew angrier still.

"Dammit all, girl, the most important man in England has asked you to be his wife. He has brought you a ring which would cost a King's ransom. Can you not look a bit more cheerful?"

"I am sorry, Papa . . . but I am doing my best to please you," Salema said.

"If that is the best you can do, you can try again!" the Earl said. "I am not such a fool as to be deceived as to why you would not go alone into my Study with Mountaired. For God's sake, girl, you are going to be his wife! It is no use looking like a frightened rabbit every time he speaks to you."

"That is exactly what . . . I am, Papa," Salema answered, "and it is . . . no use . . . expecting me to be . . . anything else."

Because he was so incensed, the Earl bent forward and gave her a sharp slap across the face.

"Just keep a civil tongue in your head," he said, "or I will punish you in a way you will find extremely unpleasant!"

Salema put her hand to her cheek, then she walked out of the Drawing-Room.

"You should not have done that, George," the Countess said quietly. "Salema is grown up and too old to be knocked about as you used to do when she was a child."

"She is too old to behave like a petulant brat!" the Earl said furiously. "If we are not careful, Mountaired will cry off, and who shall blame him? Who wants a bride who looks as if she has been left out in the rain!"

"I am sure Salema will be all right," the Countess

said. "There is no point in you working yourself up into a passion about her. It is certainly not the way to make her feel happy about her marriage."

The Earl muttered an oath under his breath, but said no more.

Only when dinner was announced did he say to the Butler:

"Where is Lady Lettice?"

"Her Ladyship asked for a tray to be sent up to her bedroom, M'Lord," the Butler replied.

The Earl would have roared with fury, but the Countess put a restraining hand on his arm.

"Perhaps it is best to leave her alone, George," she said, "and you can tell me what His Grace said about the mares. It is useless to upset Salema more than she is already."

"What she wants is a damned good hiding!" the Earl said.

At the same time, he allowed his wife to take his arm and draw him towards the Dining-Room.

*　　*　　*

Salema went to bed.

She was praying that the night would pass quickly and that Charles had been able to get the Special Licence.

She could not help being afraid that something might go wrong.

Nothing mattered so long as she could escape from the house early to-morrow morning and meet him in Monk's Wood.

As she fell asleep she was thinking only of his arms around her and his lips on hers.

Salema left the house a little earlier than she needed.

She therefore reached Monk's Wood before the sun had time to percolate through the trees.

There was still a faint mist over the magic pool.

She was standing by it, looking at the kingcups growing at the water's edge, when Charles came in sight.

Riding a fine horse, she thought he looked like a Knight going into battle.

He would save the Princess who was of course in danger of being devoured by the Dragon.

He pulled his horse to a standstill and dismounted.

She ran towards him to fling herself into his arms.

"I have missed you! Oh, Charles . . . I have missed you!" she said. "Is everything . . . all right?"

"Everything," he replied, "unless you have stopped loving me."

"How . . . could I do . . . that?" Salema asked.

He kissed her.

Then, as he drew her towards their usual seat, he said:

"I have the Special Licence, my Darling, and coming back from London I stopped at Fladbury and spoke to the Rector."

"You . . . saw him?" Salema murmured breathlessly. "And . . . he agreed to marry us?"

"He is delighted to do so! I told him I was a member of the Aired family, but as there are a great number of them, he had no idea that I was my Father's son."

"He did not . . . think it strange that you wished

. . . to be married . . . quietly?"

"I had to tell him a little white lie. I said that one of my family is old and in very bad health and that if she dies I should be in mourning and unable to marry for at least six months."

He paused before he added:

"I suppose that is very nearly true. My Grandmother is not in good health."

"But . . . she has been kind to you . . . so we do not . . . wish her to die," Salema said hastily.

"No, of course not!" Charles agreed. "She has been wonderful to me, and I am very, very fond of her."

"Will you not tell her about us?"

"I thought we might have to so that you could store your clothes there. But if she knows too much, my Father and yours will bully her into telling what she knows, and that would be a mistake."

"Y-yes . . . of course," Salema said. "I was thinking last night that all I wanted to take abroad and could not keep at home could remain with Nanny."

"I thought the same," Charles said as he smiled. "We think the same, my Darling, we are the same, and you are already a part of me."

"That is . . . what I . . . want to be," Salema said.

He kissed her possessively, and everything else was forgotten.

Then he said:

"As I do not want you to be upset or to be involved more than is necessary in the arrangements of your marriage to my Father, we will be married to-morrow afternoon, so long as you can arrange with your Nanny that we can go there after the ceremony."

"Oh, Charles . . . can we really . . . do that?"

"It is what I want to do," he said. "Then, as soon as you are agreeable, we can go abroad, where no-one can find us."

He saw as he spoke that Salema's eyes were shining.

Her face was transformed with happiness, as if there were a light within her.

He looked at her for a long moment before he said:

"If you will come with me, my Precious One, I promise it will be something you will never, ever regret."

"How could I ever regret marrying the most wonderful man in the whole world?" Salema asked.

They sat talking for only a few more minutes until Charles suggested she go immediately to see her Nanny.

"If we go through the woods and keep to the fields," he said, "I can ride with you so that you will be safe. I will wait for you and take you back home."

"I would love that." Salema smiled.

They mounted their horses and, riding as quickly as they could, reached the village of Fladbury in half-an-hour.

Salema left Charles waiting at the edge of the Wood.

Then she rode alone the short distance to her Nanny's cottage.

It was a very pretty, large cottage.

When she had retired she had lived there with her brother, who had been a School-Master.

He had died and left her the cottage.

With the pension she received from the Earl, she was, Salema knew, very comfortably off.

Salema put *Flash* into the stable.

It was actually little more than a barn at the side of the house.

Then she went in by the back door.

As she expected, Nanny was in the Kitchen preparing her breakfast.

She looked up in astonishment when she saw Salema.

"Why, Miss Salema! Is it really you? Why didn't you let me know you were coming?"

Salema kissed her.

"It is lovely to see you, Nanny," she said, "and, now that I can smell what you are cooking, I am very hungry."

"Sit down," Nanny said. "It's fortunate I went shopping yesterday afternoon."

Two minutes later she put two slices of perfectly cooked bacon and a fried egg in front of Salema.

Then she poured her out a cup of fragrant coffee.

Salema took a few mouthfuls before she said:

"I have come, Nanny, to ask for your help."

"Well, that's nothing new," Nanny replied, "and I s'pose you're in trouble with your Father again!"

"Very, very bad trouble, Nanny!"

Salema told her what had happened at Ascot.

Nanny stared at her as if she could not be hearing aright.

"Do you mean that after all that's been said between those two old gentlemen, they've made it up?"

"They have not only made it up," Salema answered, "but are using me as a token of what they believe will be a long and prosperous friendship."

In a few words she told Nanny what the Duke and her Father had planned.

"It's the most disgraceful thing I've ever heard!" Nanny expostulated. "His Grace is far too old for you and he's certainly not the sort of man as'll make you happy, seeing the way he's behaved towards his son and those in the cottages on his Estate."

Salema knew that Nanny was well aware of how much the Duke was hated locally.

"You know I cannot marry him, Nanny!" she said. "I feel sick when he touches me!"

"I'm not surprised!" Nanny said. "I can't think what your Father's about in wanting such a man to be your husband!"

"Papa admires the Duke," Salema explained, "and he knows that the feud between them has hurt him far more than it has His Grace."

Nanny pressed her lips together, and Salema knew she was well aware of this.

"In the meantime, Nanny," Salema went on, "I have fallen in love!"

She then told Nanny everything that had happened since she had met Charles, how he had saved Rufus and how they had both fallen in love with each other without knowing who they were.

Nanny sat back in her chair with a smile on her lips.

"Now, that's what I calls romantic," she said, "and it's just the way things should be!"

"But . . . you realise, Nanny, that we have to run away?"

"And the sooner the better, if you asks me!" Nanny replied.

"That is what we are going to do, and we want to know if, after we are married to-morrow afternoon, we can come and stay here with you?"

Nanny stared at her for a moment, then she laughed.

"Now, that's a surprise, I must say! But of course, dearie, you know you'll be welcome, and I'll make you as comfortable as possible, although it won't be Buckingham Palace!"

"It will be everything we want," Salema said, "and it will give us time to breathe before we go abroad, where no-one can find us."

"Well, no-one'll find you here," Nanny said. "I'll make sure of that!"

"Charles has chosen that we shall be married just after luncheon," Salema said, "because I can be with Papa in the morning. Then he will not be suspicious if he does not see me first thing in the afternoon."

"That's sensible," Nanny said, "and you know your Father often has a quick nap after lunch."

"I expect the Duke does too," Salema said, "and it is then we will slip away, get married, and come here to this dear little cottage, where I know we will be very happy."

"Of course you will," Nanny said. "I remember Master Charles when he was a little boy. Very handsome, he was. I always thought his Father was too hard on him."

"That is why he ran away," Salema said, "and that is what we are going to do now."

"If you ask me, it's the only thing you can do," Nanny said, "instead of marrying an elderly man nearly sixty. I've never heard of such a thing!"

Salema got up from the table and put her arms around Nanny's neck.

"I knew you would understand, Nanny!" she cried. "Now I will go back to Charles, who is waiting in the Wood, and tell him everything is arranged."

"You tell your young man he can always rely on me. No-one—and I mean no-one—will have any idea where you are."

"Thank you, Nanny, thank you. I knew you would not fail me!"

Salema kissed her Nanny again and hurried to take *Flash* from the stable.

Then she rode back to where Charles was waiting under the trees.

As she rode towards him he could see by the expression on her face that everything was all right.

"I thought you had forgotten about me," he said teasingly.

"I was thinking of you every moment," Salema answered, "and Nanny thinks you are doing exactly the right thing in taking me away."

"Then everything is arranged?" Charles asked in a voice of relief. "I was so afraid in case your old Nanny refused to allow herself to become involved in a plot against your Father."

"Nanny was never afraid of Papa," Salema said. "I think the truth is she was shocked by your Father and the way he treated anyone in his villages who offended him."

She saw Charles's lips tighten and knew he hated to think about it.

She made a mental note that she would not mention it again because it upset him.

"I will have to try and get some clothes over to Nanny," she said, "because, if we are very poor, we will not be able to afford new clothes when the Winter comes, especially furs and heavy coats and things like that."

"That is what I have been thinking myself," Charles said. "So I thought you might say you were giving some of your old clothes away. And if you could get them out of the house, I could drive over in a Curricle and take them to your Nanny."

"Oh, Charles, you are so clever!" Salema said. "I can easily do that because Papa bought me so many new gowns in London. I will wrap everything up in a sheet and get one of the footmen, the one who is quite half-witted and will not ask questions, to carry them down to the stables."

She paused before she went on:

"I will put them in the pony-cart and say I am taking them to the Orphanage, and meet you as you suggest."

"That is another problem solved," Charles said with satisfaction. "Really, my Darling, I think you are being very clever."

"Touch wood!" Salema cried. "Remember, anyone might betray us to your father or mine, and there are too many 'Nosey-Parkers' about, watching everything we do."

"The gods are on our side," Charles answered, "otherwise I would not have found you, my lovely one, and really, although it seems somewhat of a twisted tale, we have to thank my Father for making the man-trap into which Rufus fell."

Salema laughed.

"As you say, it is too complicated, and the only

thing that matters now is that I can get out of the man-trap which your Father and mine have set for me."

"You may be quite sure that I shall rescue you from that!" Charles replied.

They rode on until they reached Monk's Wood.

There they said good-bye and Charles explained that he was going home so as not to arouse any suspicion.

"I shall tell Papa I went riding because I could not sleep," Salema said. "I think he will understand that."

"Be as natural as you can," Charles admonished. "The only thing that matters is that you should meet me at the end of your back drive to-morrow after luncheon."

"Am I to walk there?" Salema asked.

Charles nodded.

"We have to be careful that we are not betrayed by the horses we take with us," he said. "So I am afraid, Darling, you will have to leave *Flash* and Rufus behind you."

Salema felt a little pang in her heart.

She knew she would find it hard to leave the animals she loved.

"I intend to borrow a Curricle from my Father's stable and two horses in which he is not particularly interested," Charles was saying. "I will send a message by the grooms that I am going to London and hope to be back within the course of a few days and will stay with my Grandmother. I do not think my Father will be interested, one way or the other."

"I hope not!" Salema said fervently. "And what message do I leave?"

Charles thought for a moment.

"I think you should leave a note for your Father saying that you find it impossible to marry a man who is so old, and you are therefore going away to stay with friends until the whole idea is forgotten."

"He will wonder who the 'friends' are," Salema said.

"The alternative," Charles said, "is to tell him the truth. I am not certain that would not be the best."

"The . . . truth?" Salema questioned.

"That you are running away because you cannot marry the Duke and you wish to marry someone you love and with whom you know you will be very happy."

Salema took a deep breath.

"I shall do that," she said. "I do not want to start our marriage with a lie. I will tell Papa the truth, but I am very . . . very glad that I shall . . . not be here to see how . . . angry he . . . will be!"

"You will be with me," Charles said, "and I shall not allow you to think of anything except our happiness."

He kissed her.

She rode home feeling as if her head were in the clouds and the Angels were singing.

She was no longer afraid of the future, the Duke, or her Father's anger.

The Gates of Paradise were open wide, and tomorrow she would pass through them.

chapter six

THE Church was very quiet.

There was the scent of the roses which were on the altar.

The Vicar spoke the beautiful words of the Marriage Ceremony in a deep and sincere manner.

Holding tightly on to Charles's hand, Salema thought it was the most wonderful moment in her life.

She could hardly believe that she was actually being married to the man she loved and who loved her.

* * *

Everything had gone exactly as Charles had planned.

She had ridden with her Father in the morning, and when he came back for luncheon he was in a comparatively good mood.

As soon as the meal was finished he said:

"I have some letters to write. There are members of my family who must know of your intended marriage before they read *The London Gazette*."

"You have not sent the notice yet, Papa?" Salema asked a little nervously.

"I will send it to-morrow," the Earl said, "and now I will write my letters while you get on with the lists of guests to be invited to the wedding."

Even to talk about it made the Earl feel elated.

As he left the Dining-Room he put his hand on Salema's shoulder, saying:

"You are a good girl, a very good girl, and now we will have no more nonsense. Everything will be exactly as I want it to be."

Salema did not answer.

As usual, she knew he was not thinking of her, but his own satisfaction at having the Duke as his son-in-law.

Her Mother had not come down to luncheon because she was feeling tired.

Salema thought it would therefore be easier to leave the house than it might have been.

As soon as her Father went into his Study she went up to her bedroom.

She changed from the riding-habit she had worn in the morning into a pretty gown.

It was one of the prettiest she possessed as well as the most expensive they had bought in London.

Fortunately, it was white, with a blue sash round the waist.

There was also a touch of blue beneath the *broderie anglaise* which decorated the skirt and the bodice of the gown.

"Blue for happiness!" Salema said to herself.

She managed to do up her own gown without sending for the maid.

Then she found in the cupboard the very pretty bonnet which went with it.

Trimmed with a few small curled ostrich feathers, there were blue ribbons to tie under her chin.

She looked at herself in the mirror and hoped that Charles would admire her.

Knowing the servants would now be having their midday meal, she slipped down the stairs.

She left the house by a door that was seldom used.

It took her into the shrubbery which hid the back drive from the windows at the front.

She had thought she would have to walk almost to the end of it.

But, under the first clump of trees she came to, there was Charles waiting for her.

He had a light Chaise and two young, strong-looking horses.

She knew they would carry them without any difficulty to the coast when he was ready to leave.

He stepped out of the Chaise to greet her, and she thought he was looking very smart.

His white cravat was high against his chin and tied in an intricate fashion she had not seen before.

For a moment they looked at each other.

Then he said:

"Can I really be lucky enough to marry anyone so exquisite?"

"Are we . . . really going to be . . . married?" Salema asked in a whisper.

"Now—at once!" Charles replied.

He helped her into the Chaise, and bent and kissed her.

"I love and adore you!" he said. "And when we are married I will be able to tell you how much."

They drove off, and to Salema's relief there was no-one on the back drive to see them.

There also appeared to be no-one in the few cottages they passed by at the end of the village.

The way to Fladbury was through narrow, twisting lanes.

When finally they reached it, there were no busy-bodies to be surprised when they turned in at the small drive in front of Nanny's cottage.

Charles put the horses into the stable.

Then they moved the short distance to the Church.

It was just inside the Park where there had once been an important house.

It had been burnt down at the end of the last century and never re-built.

The Church, however, was originally Norman.

Its grey stone blended with the silver birch trees that surrounded it.

There appeared to be nobody about.

But when they walked in through the door, Salema saw the Rector.

Wearing his white vestments, he was kneeling in front of the altar.

He must have heard their approach, for he rose and turned round.

Then he waited until they stood in front of him.

He opened his Prayer Book and began the Service.

To Salema, every word seemed to be spoken to her by God Himself.

When they knelt for the final Blessing, she felt that her feelings were not only caused by the sunshine coming through the stained glass windows.

There was a light so brilliant that she was sure it came from Heaven.

She knew that she and Charles had been blessed already.

They had found each other and almost by a miracle they were able to be married.

Now she was Charles's wife and no-one could take her from him.

She rose to her feet, and the Rector said in a kindly voice to Charles:

"Now you may kiss the bride."

Charles kissed her, but it was a very gentle and almost sacred kiss.

It was as if he dedicated himself to her.

Salema knew that his love not only came from his body, but from his soul.

They went into the Vestry to sign the Marriage Register.

Then the Rector said:

"May I wish you both the best of luck and great happiness in your marriage. I know that you already have the blessing of God."

"We have that because you have given it to us," Charles said, "and I can never thank you enough for making me the happiest man in the world."

The old clergyman smiled.

"That is what I hope you will always be, my son," he said. "Look after your wife and protect her because I think that is what all women need to-day."

"I will do that," Charles promised.

They left the Vestry, which was just off the Chancel.

As they walked down the aisle the Vicar again knelt in front of the altar.

Salema knew he was praying for them.

'We need all his prayers!' she thought.

They walked quickly back to the cottage the way they had come.

When they went in through the first door, Salema expected Nanny to be waiting for them.

Instead, she saw there was a note on a table.

Nanny had written:

My Dearie,

I hope you will be very happy, and I know you will want to be alone on your Wedding-Day. I've therefore gone to spend the night with my Niece, but I'll be back to get your breakfast to-morrow morning.

You'll find your Supper laid in the Kitchen and there's some rabbit soup in the Saucepan you can heat up for your husband.

My love and blessing to you both,

Nanny

Salema read the note and looked up at Charles, who was reading it too.

"Your Nanny understands what I want," he said.

He moved away from her, shut the front-door, and locked it.

Then he took her arm and started to walk up the stairs.

Salema did not say anything—she only blushed when she understood what he intended.

When they reached the landing she opened the door of the room which Nanny used for her guests.

She herself had often stayed in it.

It had previously been used by the original owner of the cottage, Nanny's brother, before he died.

It was quite a large room, although the roof sloped down to two diamond-paned windows.

They looked out over the garden.

In the centre, taking up most of the room, was a very large bed.

She saw the surprise in Charles's eyes and laughed.

"Nanny's brother," she explained, "was a very big man of over six feet, and he liked to be comfortable."

"So do I."

Charles pulled off his smart cut-away coat as he spoke and flung it on a chair.

Then he undid the blue ribbons under Salema's chin and took off her bonnet.

To her surprise, he then turned her round and started to undo the buttons of her gown.

"It is a good thing that I have had some experience in being a lady's-maid!" he teased. "You will find me quite accomplished."

"Y-you are ... making me ... jealous!" Salema said.

As her gown dropped to the ground, Charles took her in his arms.

"We have been married nearly fifteen minutes," he said, "and I have not yet properly kissed my wife!"

Then his lips were on hers and he was kissing her wildly, passionately, possessively.

She felt that she melted into his body and it was impossible to think, but only to feel.

A little later she found herself in the big bed.

The sunshine coming through the windows blinded her eyes.

Then Charles joined her and pulled her close to him.

She knew that now she was passing through the Gates of a Paradise she had thought she would never find.

He kissed her not only on her lips, but on her eyes, her neck, and her breasts.

It aroused strange sensations she did not even know existed.

The sunshine seemed to envelop her and also streak through her body like little tongues of fire.

Then, as she felt the ecstasy of his love was almost too rapturous to be borne, very gently Charles made her his.

Salema knew then that she was not only in Heaven, but a part of it.

She and Charles were indivisible and nothing could ever separate them.

*　　*　　*

A long time later, when the shadows in the garden were growing long and the sun was sinking lower in the sky, Salema said:

"Oh, Charles . . . I love you!"

"Have I made you happy, my precious one?"

"I am so happy, I feel I want to cry at the wonder of it."

"If you cry on your Wedding-day," he said, "I

shall be very offended and feel I have failed as your husband."

"How could you . . . ever do that?" Salema said. "Why did no-one tell me that love was so wonderful . . . so exciting!"

"You excite me to madness," Charles said, "as you have from the first moment I saw you. At the same time, my lovely wife, I will look after you, protect you, and try to keep you from suffering in any way, either mentally or physically."

"All that matters," Salema replied, "is that we are together. Oh, Charles . . . how can we have . . . been so . . . lucky?"

"I suppose, really," Charles said seriously, "my whole life has been leading up to this. I was not aware of it, but everywhere I went I was looking for you."

"Is that . . . true?"

"At the back of my mind," he said, "I had a picture of my ideal woman. It was something I would never have admitted to any of my friends, who would have laughed."

He paused and then continued:

"The women I met who, I admit, were sometimes very fascinating, always fell short of the woman who was in a very secret shrine in my heart, and who I began to think could not exist."

Salema drew in her breath.

"When we met . . . and you saved Rufus . . ."

"When you looked up at me I was aware of a sudden shock because you were so beautiful. Then, as if a voice were telling me, I knew I had found what I sought."

"Oh, Darling, it is so romantic!" Salema cried. "I

thought you were the most handsome man I had ever seen!"

"That is what I want you to go on thinking," Charles said, and kissed her.

Then, as he did so, a flame leapt within them both.

Once again the sun was burning in them and its light enveloped them.

*   *   *

It was late when they went downstairs to have their dinner.

Salema was wearing a beautiful *negligée* which she and her Mother had bought in Bond Street.

Charles had on a long dark robe.

They found, as Nanny had promised, that their dinner was laid very elegantly on the white linen tablecloth which covered the Kitchen table.

As Nanny was a very good cook, it was delicious.

Salema, first of all, heated up the rabbit soup, which was difficult because Charles kept kissing her.

They then ate the dishes which Nanny had prepared and left on the sideboard.

To their surprise, there was a bottle of champagne in a bucket of cold water.

"Champagne?" Charles exclaimed. "Now, where could your Nanny have got that?"

"I have no idea," Salema said. "I am sure she could not have afforded to buy it from the local Inn, even if they had anything as exotic as champagne!"

"Perhaps it is something she was keeping for a special occasion," Charles suggested.

Salema gave a cry.

"I know what it is!" she exclaimed. "I heard that, when I was christened, Papa, feeling unexpectedly generous, gave Nanny a bottle of champagne to share with the staff. I remember now Mama telling me that Nanny said:

" 'No! I shall keep it until she marries, then give it to her as a present to bring her luck!' "

Charles laughed.

"Well, it is certainly exactly what we want, and no-one could possibly give us a more welcome present than this!"

They toasted each other until Charles's kisses became more passionate and they went upstairs again.

* * *

"I do not think anyone," Salema said when the moon was shining through the windows, "could have had a happier Wedding-Day than us."

"It is the sort of wedding I have always wanted," Charles said, "and I would have hated the enormous amount of fashionable guests looking critical in the Church, and having to listen to a lot of idiotic speeches at the Reception."

Salema knew that that was what she would have had to do if she had married the Duke.

She moved a little closer to Charles.

"How . . . soon can . . . we go . . . abroad?" she asked.

"I thought, originally, to-morrow," Charles replied, "but it is so comfortable here and so peaceful that I would like to stay another night."

"So would I," Salema agreed, "and I know Nanny would be only too glad to have us."

*　　*　　*

Salema and Charles woke very late the next morning.

When they did, Salema saw there was a small piece of paper that had been thrust under the door.

Nanny had written:

> *I'm downstairs—breakfast will*
> *be ready when you are.*
>
> *Nanny*

She showed it to Charles.

"Your Nanny is the nicest woman I have ever heard of," he said, "and we will have to find a very special present to give her."

"Of course we must," Salema agreed.

At the same time, she wondered if they could afford presents for anyone.

They had not yet spoken about money, and now she said:

"I am afraid, Darling . . . I have very little money to bring . . . away with me . . . but I did bring what jewellery I possess. Some of it was left to me by my Godmothers and is quite valuable."

Charles kissed her.

"You are not to worry about that," he said. "That is my job. If we run out of money, I can find some sort of work to do. I have never failed to provide for myself in the past."

"What sort of work have you done?" Salema asked.

"Some very dirty jobs—some quite amusing

ones," he answered. "Because I am strong, there are always people who need a man to carry things for them, whether it is the cargo off a boat, luggage, or an armful of children."

Salema laughed.

"How could you have had to do that?"

"I escorted a family who had three children with them down a river in Africa. They always had to be carried ashore everywhere we stopped. They were naughty little brats. They used to pull my hair and frighten me by saying there was a crocodile beside us when it was nothing but a ripple!"

Salema laughed.

"I know what you must do," she said. "One day you must write a book, and everybody will want to read about your travels."

"I will write one about us both," Charles said, "and it will be the most exciting romance that has ever been published."

Salema was laughing as they went down to breakfast.

Salema kissed Nanny and so did Charles.

"You are exactly the sort of Nurse I ought to have had," he told her. "Instead of which I had women who were terrified of my Father and carried out all his orders—however unpleasant they might be."

"I've heard about what went on at the Castle!" Nanny said tartly. "And the sooner your forget your Father and all his goings-on, the happier you'll be!"

"You are quite right, Nanny," Charles agreed.

They sat down at the Kitchen table and ate a large breakfast while Nanny waited on them.

When they had finished they went upstairs and dressed.

"It is a terrible waste of time," Charles said. "I was thinking I could spend the whole afternoon in this comfortable bed, telling you how lovely you are."

There was an expression in his eyes which made Salema blush. Then she said:

"Before we do that, I have something to show you."

"To show me?" Charles enquired.

"It is outside, but it will not take long."

"Very well," Charles agreed, "but do not forget that this is our honeymoon."

"I am not likely to forget it," she said.

They went out of the cottage, and Salema pointed to where only a little way from them there was a small hill.

Charles had hardly noticed it before.

This part of the County was more undulating than most of his Father's Estate.

They left Nanny's cottage. At the back there was a wood of white birch trees which covered the base of the hill.

Walking beneath them with the sun coming through the leaves made Salema look very beautiful.

Charles had always thought of her as belonging to the trees.

Almost immediately they started to climb.

It was only a little sheep-track winding upwards, until Salema stopped.

"I told you, Darling," she said, "that I was prepared to live in a cave and I have brought you to see the sort of one I would like us to find."

"There is a cave here?" Charles asked, looking ahead.

"I played in it when I was a child and stayed in the cottage with Nanny when Papa and Mama went away to London or the races."

"Let me see it," Charles said good-humouredly.

A few steps took them to the cave, and it was very much larger than it looked from the opening.

Charles thought that the hill itself must go back to the time when parts of England were volcanic.

It was certainly clean, and there was rock rising in layers up to quite a high ceiling.

Charles was looking round when suddenly they heard the sound of voices.

Both he and Salema stiffened.

"We do not . . . want to be . . . seen!" she said quickly.

"No, of course not," he answered.

"Then follow me."

To his surprise, she started to climb up one side of the cave.

He realised as he looked up that there was a dark space at the top.

The voices were coming nearer.

Even as two men reached the outside of the cave, Charles managed to join Salema.

She was lying on top of the rock.

He saw there was a space of about two feet stretching out for a yard or so.

There was certainly room for them both.

As Charles lay down beside Salema, they heard the men come into the cave.

"This is a strange thing to find here," one of the newcomers remarked.

"The man Foster I was telling you about explained exactly where it was," the other man replied. "He was right in thinking that two strangers asking questions in the village might seem suspicious."

"I suppose you can trust him?" the first man remarked.

"I'm sure I can," the other replied. "Apparently, he was extremely badly treated by the Duke and is determined to get his revenge."

Salema felt Charles's body which was close against her stiffen.

She wondered what could be happening.

"Well, everything depends on him," the second man remarked, "and if he lets us down, we'll be in trouble."

"I'm sure he won't do that."

The man who had spoken gave an exclamation, saying:

"Here he comes, and you can see for yourself what you think of him."

The man referred to as "Foster" came into the cave.

The moment he spoke Salema knew he had a Hertfordshire accent and was local.

" 'Afternoon, Sirs," Foster said. "Oi thinks as 'ow you'd find th' cave right enough."

"We found it," the first man said, "and now I want you to tell my friend exactly what you told me."

"Tis not difficult," Foster answered. "Oi'll take ye later, when it's dark, to th' Castle. Oi'll let ye in through a broken window on the Ground Floor which only Oi knows about."

"I understand it's a year or two since the Duke dismissed you," the second man said. "How can you be sure the window isn't mended?"

"Because Oi 'ad a peep at it two nights ago after Oi met th' gentleman here," Foster said. "Oi'm not daft!"

"No, of course not!" the first man said soothingly. "And when we've got inside—what do we do then?"

"Depends what ye're a-looking for," Foster answered. "There's some fine pictures in th' Study— some Frenchie ones, Oi thinks, in th' Drawing-Room, an' what Oi've always heard tell are real valuable be 'em in th' Library."

"Those are the Rubens and Van Dycks," the first man said, speaking to his friend.

"Those are the ones I want."

"Right," Foster said. "Oi'll take ye to th' Library an' mind yer hurries with what ye're taking, 'cos us don't want to get caught."

"No, of course not, and we are very grateful to you, Foster. You shall have a very generous remuneration as soon as the pictures are in our hands."

"If ye meet Oi in th' orchard," Foster said, "which be on th' left side of th' garden, at midnight Oi'll take ye where ye want t' go."

"Thank you," the first man replied.

"Now, Oi'll be goin' back the way Oi come," Foster went on, "an' ye gentlemen walk left when ye leave th' cave an' come down in a different direction. Us don't want no-one t'see us!"

"That's for sure!" the second man answered. "And we'll meet you to-night."

"T'night, after twelve o'clock," Foster repeated. "An' ye won't forget to bring th' money with ye?"

"No, of course not," the first man said reassuringly.

"Roight then—cheerio!" Foster said.

Listening, hardly daring to breathe, Salema heard him leave the cave.

A few seconds later the two other men did the same.

Neither she nor Charles moved until there was no chance of any of the three returning.

Then, slowly without speaking, Charles climbed down from the top of the rock.

He lifted Salema down after him.

Holding on to him, she asked in a whisper:

"What are we going to do?"

"We will go back to the cottage first, before we even talk about it," Charles replied.

They hurried back the way they had come.

When they were inside the cottage, Salema went to Nanny's Sitting-Room which was on the right-hand-side of the door.

It was a comfortable room with Nanny's sewing-basket by the fireplace.

A portrait of Salema, which had been executed by a local artist when she was aged five, hung over the mantelpiece.

Charles shut the door behind him.

She turned towards him and he put his arms around her.

"What are . . . we to . . . do?" she asked. "What can we . . . do?"

"One thing we have to prevent," Charles said, "is them taking away the Rubens, which is extremely valuable, or any of the Van Dycks, which are all of my ancestors."

"I know," Salema said, "but how can you tell . . . your Father what is . . . going to . . . happen?"

"I am not going to tell my Father," Charles replied.

"You cannot . . . tackle those . . . three men . . . alone."

"No, I am not so stupid as to try," Charles agreed. "But I can manage with one other man to help me."

Salema gave a cry and put her arms round him.

"They . . . might hurt . . . you!"

"I doubt it," Charles answered. "They are not likely to carry weapons, because then they would undoubtedly be hanged. If they are unarmed, it is merely a case of transportation."

"They will not like that, but—who is Foster?"

"I am sure I remember Foster," Charles said. "I think he was a footman. Of course, if he was dismissed, as they said, it would be a stigma against him for the rest of his life. It would be difficult for him to get another job."

"So he has a grudge!"

"Apparently a very large one!" Charles agreed.

He walked across the room and back as if he was thinking, then said:

"I will leave you here with Nanny—"

"No!" Salema interrupted. "I will not be left behind."

She stopped with a sigh and then continued:

"Oh, Charles, how can you think that I would let you go into danger and not be there with you? If you insist on stopping these men from stealing your pictures . . . then I am coming too."

She expected Charles to argue, but to her surprise, he laughed.

"I suppose," he said, "that is exactly what I expected you to say. We shall be in some tight corners and meet some difficult situations when we go round the world, and so, my precious little love, we might as well get used to facing them together."

"That is exactly what we . . . will do," Salema said, "but, Charles . . . I am very . . . frightened!"

"It is certainly something I did not expect to happen on the first day of our honeymoon!" Charles exclaimed. "But I suppose we should think it was lucky that we happened to be in the cave when Foster met the men who have obviously come down from London in order to rob my Father."

There was silence until Salema asked:

"Do you think perhaps . . . we could prevent the men from stealing . . . then slip away . . . come back here . . . and leave to-morrow . . . as you intended?"

"That is exactly what I am planning to do," Charles answered, "and if I tie them up and leave them in charge of Goddard, you and I should be able to keep out of the picture."

"Who is Goddard?" Salema asked.

"He is my Father's Head Groom," Charles answered. "He is a young man, but because the old groom died, he got the position far sooner than he expected."

"And you can . . . trust him?"

"He has always been on my side," Charles replied. "When he was a stable-boy he would always saddle me the best horse when the Head Groom would not let me ride him."

Charles paused, then went on:

"When I told him I wanted two strong horses and it would be better if my Father did not enquire

138

what had happened to them, he assured me no-one would realise they had left the stables!"

"He sounds just the man . . . we want!"

"He is taller than I am," Charles said, "and I should think as strong, if not stronger!"

Salema gave a little laugh.

"You are making me feel sorry for those men from London, and Foster, who has obviously been badly treated."

"Do not feel too sorry for them," Charles remarked. "They must learn to leave other people's belongings alone, or face the consequences."

He held out his arm, and Salema moved close to him.

"Now," Charles said, "we can be together until it is getting on for midnight—and I have a great deal to say to you."

"What . . . do you want to . . . tell me?" Salema asked.

"That I love you!" Charles replied. "And that is more important than all the pictures in the world!"

chapter seven

DINNER was very late because Charles would not
let Salema get dressed.

After he had told her what he planned for later
in the evening, he had taken her upstairs and into
the big bed.

"Forget everything, the endless difficulties and
the thieving," he said. "This is our honeymoon."

He kissed her until once again the sun burned
within them both.

It was so perfect, so exactly what she had
longed for that Salema did forget everything except
Charles.

When the shadows began to grow longer and
the sun sank toward the horizon, she said to him
softly:

"Must we . . . worry about the . . . pictures?"

"They are part of the heritage my children will
have," Charles answered, "especially my son."

She moved a little closer to him.

"I want to . . . have a son," she said, "who is

as . . . handsome and . . . wonderful as . . . you."

"That is what I want, too," Charles said, "but I am afraid, my Darling, we will not be able to afford children for a long time."

She knew he was thinking that his Father was still a comparatively young man.

"Money does not count," she answered. "The children will fit into our cave when we find it, and because we will love them as we love each other they will be very happy."

"I know that," Charles said.

He kissed her passionately.

He thought that only Salema would believe they could be completely happy in a cave and that money did not matter.

At the same time, because she was so beautiful he wanted to dress her in gold and silver and put jewels round her neck.

He knew, however, it was no use saying so.

They had to live on the small allowance his Grandmother gave him and what he could earn.

'We will survive,' he told himself, looking at the crimson sky outside the windows, 'and what really matters is that we will be together.'

He felt as if the words were written on the walls around him.

He knew they were written in his heart.

"I love you!" he said.

He wondered why there were no other words to express what he was feeling.

The love he had for Salema and she for him was, as she believed, part of the Divine.

During the Marriage Service he had felt that God blessed them, that He would therefore look after them and they could always depend on Him.

They were thoughts he had not had before.

Even when he had been so unhappy as a child he could not believe in the God his Mother had talked to him about.

She had said that He was merciful and would always take care of him.

He had felt that if God really did care, He would have protected him from his Father's endless lectures, beatings, and rages.

Yet now, because he had found Salema, he believed fervently that God was merciful.

Salema moved a little closer to him.

"I . . . I am . . . frightened," she said. "If you do prevent these men from stealing . . . will you not have to give evidence against them . . . so that we cannot . . . go abroad?"

"I have thought of that," Charles replied, "but I did not want to talk about it in case it upset you."

He knew she was anticipating that their Fathers might learn that they were married.

The Duke would rage at them.

Also Salema thought with a little shudder that her Father would be furiously angry.

"What we are going to do," Charles said quietly, "is to drive from here up to the stables of the Castle when I am sure everybody will have gone to bed."

Salema was listening as he went on:

"I will find Goddard, tell him what is happening, and also inform him that he is to be the Hero of the Day."

"How can that be?" Salema asked.

"When we have tied up the robbers," Charles explained, "he will take all the credit for preventing them from stealing the pictures."

"You mean . . . we will not . . . be there?" Salema questioned.

"As soon as they are unable to do any more harm," Charles replied, "you and I will slip away and come back here."

"Oh, Charles . . . that is a wonderful . . . plan!" Salema cried.

"Then we will leave to-morrow, as I intended," he added.

She put her arm round his neck and pulled his head down to hers.

"That is what I want," she said, "and we will find our cave somewhere abroad, where no-one will find us, and where we will be very, very happy."

"That is what we will do," Charles agreed.

He kissed her wildly and fiercely, as if he were afraid of losing her.

She felt her body respond to him.

Also he seemed to draw her heart from between her lips and make it his.

It was so wonderful that Salema felt the Angels were singing overhead.

As the sun disappeared, the first evening star sparkled in the sky.

Salema felt it was a portent that all would be well and she need not be afraid.

Charles was the Knight she thought would kill all the Dragons.

"How can he be so marvellous?" she asked.

Then the rapture of their love burst into flames.

*   *   *

Nanny had prepared a delicious dinner for them.

Salema knew that she could not have afforded to buy the delicious ingredients.

She had, however, seen Charles put a gold coin into Nanny's hand before they had set out to explore the cave.

Charles was hungry.

Although she did not wish to disappoint Nanny, Salema was too happy to eat very much.

They finished what was left of the champagne.

Nanny confirmed that it was the bottle she had put away after Salema's christening.

"You must have been clairvoyant," Salema said, "because it was just what we wanted!"

Nanny was delighted that they appreciated her food and the champagne.

It, however, worried her when she realised they intended to leave the cottage late at night.

"Why can't you rest while you've got the chance?" she queried.

"We have something very important to do, Nanny," Charles explained, "but we will be back as quickly as we can, so leave the door unlocked and go to bed."

"I can't think what mischief you two are up to," Nanny remarked.

Salema, however, knew she would do as they asked.

It was after half-past-ten when Charles, having put the two horses between the shafts, drove out of the small drive.

There was a full moon so that they could see their

145

way clearly through the twisting lanes which led to the Castle.

It would have been, Salema knew, a shorter distance if they had ridden over the fields.

She wondered if that was what the robbers intended to do.

They approached the Castle by the back drive.

When they reached the stables, Charles told her to hold the reins while he went and woke up Goddard.

The Head Groom had a small house at the end of the stable-yard.

As it happened, Goddard had not gone to bed.

He was doing some accounts in his Kitchen.

He was surprised to see Charles, who he thought was in London.

When Charles told him what was happening, he was horrified.

"Oi remembers that young Foster," he said. "Nasty bit o' work, 'e were. Oi weren't surprised when 'Is Grace give 'im the sack. At the same time, 'e was real 'ard on the boy which meant 'e weren't able to get another job."

Charles thought it was the usual way his Father behaved, but he did not say so.

"What we have to do, Goddard," he said, "is to save the pictures. We must tie up the men so that they cannot escape, while you fetch the Police."

Goddard nodded and Charles went on:

"I want you to promise you will not say that I was there. I am going abroad to-morrow and do not wish to be involved in the proceedings which are inevitable when the men come up for trial."

Goddard stared at him.

"Ye means, M'Lord, Oi'm to say Oi done it sin-gle-'anded like?"

"It is something of which you are quite capable," Charles answered.

Goddard laughed.

"Oi 'opes Oi'll not disappoint ye, M'Lord."

"You will not do that," Charles replied, "and if you have the key to the back door, you can let me into the Castle. After you have put the horses into the stable, join me in the Library."

They came out together into the yard.

Salema was aware that Goddard was surprised to see her.

He did not say anything but only started to take the horses from between the shafts.

He had given Charles the key to the back door and, taking Salema by the hand, they walked towards it.

The staff, who were getting on in years, had retired to bed early.

Charles was aware of this.

The stone-floored passage of the Kitchen quarters were empty and silent.

They passed the Pantry.

They could hear the snores of the footman who slept there in order to guard the safe in which the silver was kept.

It was dark, but Charles knew every inch of the way.

He drew Salema through the long corridors with only an occasional lighted sconce.

Finally they reached the Library, which was at the other end of the Castle.

Salema had never seen it before.

Charles had taken a candle from one of the sconces on the wall outside.

He lit a candelabrum which stood on a table near the mantelpiece.

It was then she looked up and saw the Rubens which the robbers intended to steal.

It was beautiful and exquisitely painted.

She could understand why Charles was determined that it should not be taken from the Castle he would one day inherit.

This wall was the only one in the Library that was not covered by books.

Salema could see that the portraits on either side of the fireplace were of Charles's ancestors.

They had all been painted by Van Dyck.

They were very attractive, one in particular, who she learned later was Charles's great-great-grandfather, to whom he bore a distinct resemblance.

It had been painted when he had been the Marquis of Aired and it included his dogs.

It made her think of Rufus.

There was a little pang in her heart when she knew that after to-morrow she might never see him again.

He would be perfectly safe and well-looked-after because her Mother was very fond of him.

At the same time, Salema knew that he would miss her.

She did not, however, have time to look round, for Charles said in a low voice:

"Come with me."

It was the first time he had spoken since they had entered the Castle.

Having left the Library, they went along another corridor.

It took them to what Salema knew, as soon as she saw it, was the Gun-Room.

There were guns of every sort and description against the walls.

Beneath them were the drawers in which were kept the bullets to fit them, and the powder horns.

There were also fishing-rods.

On another wall there were ancient swords which must have been used by Charles's ancestors in olden times.

Charles put the candle he was carrying down on a table.

Taking a duelling pistol from its box, he began priming and loading it.

"I want one too," Salema said.

Charles looked at her in astonishment.

"I will protect you."

"I want to protect . . . you," Salema answered. "Actually, I am a very good shot. Papa taught me when I was quite young and, because he had no son, I was allowed to go out shooting with him when I was older."

She smiled and added:

"I even had a small gun of my own, although I really do not like killing anything."

Charles bent forward and kissed her lips.

"That is what I would expect you to say," he said, "but if it will make you any happier, I will give you a pistol. But you must be careful and promise not to fire it unless it is absolutely necessary—which I hope it will not be!"

"I promise," Salema said.

She was thinking that by a terrible chance something might go wrong.

If the three men were stronger than Charles and Goddard, at least she might be able to help them.

It was, however, extremely unlikely.

Charles put down his duelling pistol.

Opening a drawer, he took out the smallest pistol Salema had ever seen.

"This is the one my Grandmother used to carry when she went on long journeys before she married," he explained, "because some of her relatives lived in the North of England."

"Why did she want it?" Salema asked.

"She told me," Charles replied, "that she was terrified of Highwaymen and was determined to protect herself if she was held up by one."

"I think your Grandmother was absolutely right," Salema said, "and that is another thing I admire about her."

Charles knew Salema was thinking of how his Grandmother had always taken his part against the Duke.

Also how fortunate he had been to have her money so that he could be independent after his Father had cut him off without a penny.

He primed and loaded the small pistol and handed it to Salema.

"Be careful with it, my precious love," he said. "Do not shoot me by mistake!"

"How could you think I would do anything so awful?" she asked. "But I promise you, Darling, I will be very, very careful."

Charles picked up the duelling pistol and the candle.

"Come along," he said, "we must get into position."

They went back to the Library and found Goddard there, waiting for them.

When he saw the duelling pistol in Charles's hand he remarked:

"That's wise, M'Lord, it's always best t'be prepared!"

"I doubt if the men will be armed," Charles said. "At the same time, if I have something with which to threaten them, it will make it easier for you to tie them up."

From the candle he was carrying he lit the candles of two gold candlesticks.

They stood at either end of the mantelpiece.

Then he blew out those he had lit in the candelabrum when they had first arrived.

Now parts of the large room were almost in darkness.

Charles said to Goddard:

"I think from what I heard they will come in through the door, having been let into the house through one of the windows on the lower Ground Floor."

Goddard nodded.

Charles, taking Salema by the hand, drew her to a window at the far end of the Library which was almost in complete darkness.

"You, my Precious," he said to her in a voice that only she could hear, "are to stay behind the curtain and, while you can peep through, whatever happens, it would be a mistake for you to be seen."

"Y-yes . . . of course," Salema agreed.

Charles went behind the curtain with her and kissed her tenderly before he said:

"Do not be frightened. We will leave as soon as this unpleasantness is over."

Salema put her arms round his neck.

"Promise . . . promise me you will be . . . careful?"

"Because I want more than anything else in the world to tell you of my love," Charles replied, "I promise you I will take every care."

She knew what he was implying, and she blushed.

He kissed her again very gently, then went back into the room.

He placed Goddard behind a big bookcase where he could not be seen when anyone first entered.

He himself took up position behind the curtains of the nearest window to the bookcase.

Then there was an eerie silence while they waited.

There was nothing to be heard but the faint ticking of the clock on the mantelpiece.

Salema was afraid for Charles.

She was also afraid that they might not get away to-morrow.

She could not help wishing she had not taken him up to the cave which had delighted her as a child.

If they had left to-morrow morning as they had originally intended, they would not have learned for a long time that the Rubens was missing, also that perhaps three of the Van Dycks had been taken away.

Then she told herself that, underneath Charles's desire to be free of his Father, was an ingrained pride.

He belonged to a great family.

The Aireds were part of the History of England.

'He will save his pictures, then there will be no further worries,' she told herself.

She peeped through the crack in the curtains, hoping she could see Charles.

Then she was aware that silently, so that she had not heard a sound, the door of the Library was opening.

She held her breath.

She saw a head looking cautiously through the aperture and thought it was Foster.

He opened the door wider.

Then he and two men following him were in the Library.

By the light of the two candles on the mantelpiece Salema could see that they were both unpleasant-looking.

One of them was broad-shouldered and looked strong, but his face, she thought, was that of a criminal.

Slowly and silently they walked towards the fireplace.

They stared up at the Rubens that hung over it.

As they did so, Charles and Goddard came out from their hiding places.

"May I enquire what you are doing here in the Castle?" Charles asked.

There was an audible gasp from Foster as the men turned round.

Charles walked towards them with his duelling pistol in his hand.

It was then the largest of the three men made a dash for the door.

Goddard caught hold of him and threw him down on the floor.

The other man from London was then tackled by Charles.

To Salema's consternation, he put his duelling pistol down on a table and went at him with his fists up, like a pugilist.

The man tried to strike back at him.

It was, however, obvious that Charles was the more experienced fighter of the two.

He caught the man a heavy blow on the point of the chin.

It lifted the robber off the ground before he crashed backwards, unconscious.

Charles reached for the ropes.

Salema realised Goddard had put them down on the seat of an armchair.

Charles started to tie the rope round the unconscious man's body.

As he did so, she saw with horror that Foster had drawn a long, sharp knife from inside his coat.

He raised his arm.

She knew he was going to stab Charles in the back.

Without pausing for thought, knowing that Charles was in deadly danger, she fired her small pistol.

With brilliant accuracy she shot Foster in the wrist.

As the sound of the shot exploded through the Library, he gave a loud scream.

Dropping his knife, Foster sank to the floor, groaning.

The man fighting Goddard looked round at the sound of the explosion.

This enabled Goddard to throw him onto the ground.

Then he gave him a blow on the head which rendered him unconscious.

Just as Charles was doing, he seized the rope and started to tie the man up.

Without really meaning to, Salema came from her hiding-place.

Her eyes were on Charles, knowing she had saved him.

At the same time, she was still afraid he might be in danger.

Blood was pouring from Foster's wrist and he began whimpering:

"Oi'm dyin'! Oi'm dyin'! 'Elp me!"

Nobody paid him any attention.

Charles had almost completed tying up his robber and was encircling the rope around his ankles.

He pulled the knot tight.

Even as he did so, the door of the Library opened and the Duke walked in.

Behind him were his valet and the Nightfootman who had been on duty in the Hall.

The Duke was wearing a long robe over his nightshirt.

For a moment he just stared at the men lying on the floor.

Then he asked in a voice of fury:

"What the devil's going on here?"

Because he was nearest to the Duke, Goddard replied:

"Robbers, Yer Grace! They were after Yer Grace's pictures."

"My pictures?" the Duke exclaimed. "Who the hell let them in?"

It was Charles who answered his Father.

He pointed to Foster, who was clutching his bleeding wrist and said:

"It was Foster, Father, who was getting his own back because you dismissed him."

"That snivelling little swine?" the Duke raged. "Are you telling me that he dared to let these thieves into the Castle in order to steal my pictures? God knows, I will have him hanged for this and his accomplices with him!"

"Oi ain't 'urt anyone—Oi' ain't 'urt anyone!" Foster screamed.

"You will be hanged by the neck," the Duke raged, "and I will make sure of it."

He spoke so violently that almost as if he had told him to do so, Foster staggered to his feet.

"Oi wishes Oi'd killed ye!" he shouted. "Ye're cruel an' 'eartless an' everyone hates ye! It's ye as should die—not Oi!"

Foster spat the words at the Duke, who walked forward, his face contorted with fury.

As he reached Foster he raised his arm to strike him.

Foster screamed.

For a moment the Duke seemed to stiffen.

Then he stood completely still, as if he were turned to stone.

Suddenly he crashed forward onto the ground.

He fell half on top of the man Charles had roped while he was unconscious.

Because she was so frightened, Salema put out her hand to hold on to Charles.

It was then that he took command.

He, the valet, and the footman lifted the Duke, who was unconscious, onto the sofa.

Then he said to Goddard:

"Ride at once for the Doctor."

" 'Course, M'Lord," Goddard agreed.

He ran from the Library.

Charles looked at the footman and the valet.

"Take Foster to the back premises," he ordered. "Lock him up so that he cannot escape, although he is not likely to get far."

The two men moved to obey him.

Charles looked again at his Father lying still before he put out his hand to Salema.

She moved against him and he realised she was trembling.

"It is all right, my Precious," he said quietly. "But you understand I must deal with all this, so I want you to go upstairs to bed."

She looked up at him in surprise, and he said:

"I will join you just as soon as I can."

He took her by the hand and led her out of the Library.

They went into the Hall and up the great staircase.

As Charles reached the room in which he had been sleeping while he was at the Castle, he realised it was in darkness.

He took a lighted candle from one of the sconces in the corridor.

Walking into the room, he lit the candles on the dressing-table and a small candelabrum by the bed.

Then he put his arms round Salema.

"Oh . . . Charles," she whispered, "w-what will . . . happen now?"

"Leave everything to me, my Darling," he said. "Just undress, climb into bed, and lie quietly until I can come to you."

"You . . . will be . . . all right?" she asked in a sudden panic.

"Perfectly all right, thanks to you," he said. "You saved my life, my Precious, as you promised you would. But you understand I have a great deal to see to before I can be with you as I want to be."

He left her before she could say anything, closing the door softly behind him.

She felt suddenly weak after all that had happened.

She took off her gown and got into bed.

She felt a little shy with only her silk chemise to wear.

'We will sleep here to-night,' she thought, 'but I am sure we . . . will be able to . . . leave in the . . . morning.'

Somehow, however, she knew it was unlikely.

She was afraid, not only for Charles, but for their future.

* * *

It was a long time, in fact over two hours, before the door opened and Charles came in.

Salema sat up.

"I am sorry I have been so long," he said in a quiet voice, "but we had to get my Father up to bed. Now the Doctor has seen him and he has also attended, although he does not deserve it, to Foster's wrist."

"I . . . I had to . . . shoot him," Salema said. "He was going . . . to knife you in the . . . back."

"I thought that was why you did it," Charles replied, "and I am very grateful that you stopped him from injuring me. I very stupidly did not think he would carry an offensive weapon."

As he was talking, he pulled back the curtains.

Salema could see the moon and the stars which filled the sky.

Charles undressed and got into bed.

He took Salema in his arms.

"It is all right, my sweet lovely little wife," he said. "I will not have you frightened. It was very brave and very clever of you to shoot Foster in the wrist."

Salema gave a little sob.

"He . . . might have . . . hurt you!" she said. "Please, Charles . . . can we . . . go away . . . to-morrow?"

There was a note of desperation in her voice that he did not miss.

He replied quietly:

"I am afraid, my Precious Love, that that is impossible."

"Oh, Charles . . . !"

"The Doctor has examined my Father," Charles explained, "and he has suffered a very bad stroke. In fact, Dr. Grey, whom I have known since I was a boy and in whom I have complete confidence, expects that my Father will not regain consciousness and will die during the night. He is therefore staying here beside his bed."

Salema could hardly believe it.

Then she said in a hesitating voice:

"If . . . if he . . . dies . . . then we . . . cannot go . . . away."

"Not for the moment," Charles agreed, "but I promise you, my Darling, that we will not be defrauded of our honeymoon and we will go away together the moment it is possible."

He pulled her a little closer to him before he said:

"It will certainly be a more comfortable journey than I anticipated, and I will be able to show you all the beautiful places I want to do, but now we will be able to do it in style."

He smiled down at her before he added:

"I will not have to worry about you being uncomfortable, or regretting that you married me."

"You . . . know I will . . . never regret . . . that," Salema murmured. "But it is all so . . . bewildering . . . I cannot believe it has . . . happened."

"But it has!" Charles said. "And from now on, my Darling, our lives will be very different from what I expected they would be."

Then Salema knew exactly what he meant.

He would be a Duke, a very rich and powerful man.

She thought to herself that it did not really matter as long as they were together.

She felt Charles's hand moving over her skin.

Despite everything, she felt a little thrill within her breast, and she said:

"I did . . . want to . . . show you that we . . . could be . . . happy in a cave . . . however small . . . however . . . primitive."

"I think, my Lovely One," Charles said, "when we

160

are alone at night, as we are now, wherever we are, in a room large or small, furnished or unfurnished, it will be a Cave of Love."

"That is . . . true," Salema whispered happily. "I will . . . love you, and . . . love you and . . . nothing, however . . . frightening or upsetting . . . can alter . . . that."

"Of course it cannot!" Charles agreed. "And although our future will be very different from what I intended, there will be a great many things for us to do, my Precious, which I know you will enjoy. The first, of course, being to get rid of the man-traps."

Because it was something she had not expected him to say, Salema gave a little choked laugh.

"Oh, Charles . . . that will be wonderful . . . and if we are to . . . live here I can have . . . Rufus and *Flash* . . . with me."

"Of course," Charles agreed.

Because she could not help it, Salema felt the tears come into her eyes.

It was as if everything were fitting into place like a jig-saw puzzle.

"You do realise," Charles went on quietly, "that we now have no reason to hide or to be afraid of people finding us?"

There was a hint of laughter in his voice as he added:

"After all, your Father will be delighted! He wanted you to marry the Duke of Mountaired, and that, my Darling, is exactly what you have done."

Salema wanted to laugh, but the tears were running down her cheeks.

They were tears of happiness, and relief.

Also, Charles realised, tears of shock after all she had gone through.

He kissed the tears away.

Then, as he kissed her lips, her neck, and her breasts, she felt little flames rippling through her.

How was it possible to think of the past, the present, or the future, when Charles was making love to her?

The Light which had blinded her before, the Light which came from Heaven, enveloped them both.

Nothing mattered except that they were alone together in their Cave of Love.

It was theirs now, and for all eternity.

ABOUT THE AUTHOR

Barbara Cartland, the world's most famous romantic novelist, who is also an historian, playwright, lecturer, political speaker and television personality, has now written over 570 books and sold over 600 million copies all over the world.

She has also had many historical works published and has written four autobiographies as well as the biographies of her mother and that of her brother, Ronald Cartland, who was the first Member of Parliament to be killed in the last war. This book has a preface by Sir Winston Churchill and has just been published with an introduction by the late Sir Arthur Bryant.

"Love at the Helm," a novel written with the help and inspiration of the late Earl Mountbatten of Burma, Great Uncle of His Royal Highness The Prince of Wales, is being sold for the Mountbatten Memorial Trust.

She has broken the world record for the last seventeen years by writing an average of twenty three books a year. In the Guinness Book of World

Records she is listed as the world's top-selling author.

In 1978 she sang an Album of Love Songs with the Royal Philharmonic Orchestra.

In private life Barbara Cartland, who is a Dame of Grace of the Order of St John of Jerusalem, Chairman of the St John Council in Hertfordshire and Deputy President of the St John Ambulance Brigade, has fought for better conditions and salaries for Midwives and Nurses.

She championed the cause for the Elderly in 1956, invoking a Government Enquiry into the "Housing Conditions of Old People."

In 1962 she had the Law of England changed so that Local Authorities had to provide camps for their own Gypsies. This has meant that since then thousands and thousands of Gypsy children have been able to go to School which they had never been able to do in the past, as their caravans were moved every twenty four hours by the Police.

There are now fourteen camps in Hertfordshire and Barbara Cartland has her own Romany Gypsy Camp called Barbaraville by the Gypsies.

Her designs "Decorating with Love" are being sold all over the USA and the National Home Fashions League made her in 1981, "Woman of Achievement."

Barbara Cartland's book "Getting Older, Growing Younger" has been published in Great Britain and the USA and her fifth Cookery Book, "The Romance of Food" is now being used by the House of Commons.

In 1984 she received at Kennedy Airport, America's Bishop Wright Air Industry Award for her contribution to the development of aviation. In 1931 she and two RAF Officers thought of, and carried, the first aeroplane-towed glider air-mail.

During the War she was Chief Lady Welfare Officer in Bedfordshire looking after 20,000 Service men and women. She thought of having a pool of Wedding Dresses at the War Office so a Service Bride could hire a gown for the day.

She bought 1,000 secondhand gowns without coupons for the ATS, the WAAFS and the WRENS. In 1945 Barbara Cartland received the Certificate of Merit from Eastern Command.

In 1964 Barbara Cartland founded the National Association for Health of which she is the President, as a front for all the Health Stores and for any product made as alternative medicine.

This has now a £500,000,000 turnover a year, with one third going in export.

In January 1988 she received "La Medaille de Vermeil de la Ville de Paris," (The Gold Medal of Paris). This is the highest award to be given by the City of Paris for Achievement—25 million books sold in France.

In March 1988 Barbara Cartland was asked by the Indian Government to open their Health Resort outside Delhi. This is almost the largest Health Resort in the world.

Barbara Cartland was received with great enthusiasm by her fans, who also fêted her at a Reception in the city and she received the gift of an embossed plate from the Government.

Barbara Cartland was made a Dame of the Order of the British Empire in the 1991 New Year's

Honours List, by Her Majesty The Queen for her contribution to literature and for her work for the Community.

Dame Barbara has now written the greatest number of books by a British author passing the 564 books written by John Creasy.

AWARDS

1945   Received Certificate of Merit, Eastern Command, for being Welfare Officer to 5,000 troops in Bedfordshire.

1953   Made a Commander of the Order of St. John of Jerusalem. Invested by H.R.H. The Duke of Gloucester at Buckingham Palace.

1972   Invested as Dame of Grace of the Order of St. John in London by The Lord Prior, Lord Cacia.

1981   Received "Achiever of the Year" from the National Home Furnishing Association in Colorado Springs, U.S.A., for her designs for wallpaper and fabrics.

1984   Received Bishop Wright Air Industry Award at Kennedy Airport, for inventing the aeroplane-towed Glider.

1988   Received from Monsieur Chirac, The Prime Minister, The Gold Medal of the City of Paris, at the Hotel de la Ville, Paris, for selling 25 million books and giving a lot of employment.

1991   Invested as Dame of the Order of The British Empire, by H.M. The Queen at Buckingham Palace for her contribution to Literature.

Called after her own beloved Camfield Place, each Camfield Novel of Love by Barbara Cartland is a thrilling, never-before published love story by the greatest romance writer of all time.

Barbara Cartland